# TORMENTED LOVE

## A CHRISTIAN ROMANCE

## JULIETTE DUNCAN

BOOK 3 "THE TRUE LOVE SERIES"

Cover Design by http://www.StunningBookCovers.com

Copyright © 2016 Juliette Duncan

All rights reserved

# PRAISE FOR "TORMENTED LOVE"

"Real issues, real solutions. I've read every book in this series so far, and can't wait for the next. I love that it deals with real life issues and shows that healing and changes take time (too often we look for quick fixes.)" *Val*

"Juliette Duncan has done it again. Tormented Love is a good title for this 3rd book, as Ben, Tessa and Jayden struggle with situations and decisions that life throws at them." *Shirley*

"Wonderful story kept me captivated looking forward to the continued journey of all the characters hoping for a wonderful and thank you for the journey and thank you for the wonderful lessons I'm learning of trusting God." *Amazon Customer*

"3 rd book in this series. The story is so real. I can not wait to find out what happens in book 4.." *Nancy*

## ALSO BY JULIETTE DUNCAN

**Find all of Juliette Duncan's books on her website:**
www.julietteduncan.com/library

### True Love Series
*Tender Love*
*Tested Love*
*Tormented Love*
*Triumphant Love*

### Precious Love Series
*Forever Cherished*
*Forever Faithful*
*Forever His*

### Water's Edge Series
*When I Met You*
*Because of You*
*With You Beside Me*
*All I Want is You*
*It Was Always You*
*My Heart Belongs to You*

### A Sunburned Land Series
A mature-age romance series
*Slow Road to Love*
*Slow Path to Peace*
*Slow Ride Home*

*Slow Dance at Dusk*
*Slow Trek to Triumph*
*Christmas at Goddard Downs*

**The Shadows Series**
A jilted teacher, a charming Irishman, & the chance to escape
their pasts & start again.
*Lingering Shadows*
*Facing the Shadows*
*Beyond the Shadows*
*Secrets and Sacrifice*
*A Highland Christmas*

**A Time For Everything Series**
A mature-age Christian Romance series
*A Time to Treasure*
*A Time to Care*
*A Time to Abide*
*A Time to Rejoice*

**Transformed by Love Christian Romance Series**
*Because We Loved*
*Because We Forgave*
*Because We Dreamed*
*Because We Believed*
*Because We Cared*

**Billionaires with Heart Series**
*Her Kind-Hearted Billionaire*
*Her Generous Billionaire*

*Her Disgraced Billionaire*
*Her Compassionate Billionaire*

**The Potter's House Books...**
**Stories of hope, redemption, and second chances.**
*The Homecoming*
*Unchained*
*Blessings of Love*
*The Hope We Share*
*The Love Abounds*
*Love's Healing Touch*
*Melody of Love*
*Whispers of Hope*
*Promise of Peace*

**Heroes Of Eastbrooke Christian Suspense Series**
*Safe in His Arms*
*Under His Watch*
*Within His Sight*
*Freed by His Love*

**Stand Alone Christian Romantic Suspense**
*Leave Before He Kills You*

**The Madeleine Richards Series**
Although the 3 book series is intended mainly for pre-teen/Middle Grade girls, it's been read and enjoyed by people of all ages.

# CHAPTER 1

 risbane, Australia

TESSA HELD her breath as Ben, her husband of less than a year, punched redial for the fifth time in less than an hour. She prayed that Jayden, his teenage son, would pick up this time. A muscle in Ben's jaw twitched as he stared vacantly out the living room window, his chest heaving with measured breaths. When the phone diverted to Jayden's voicemail, Ben hung up without leaving a message. He'd already left more than they could count.

She slipped her arms around Ben's waist from behind and leaned her head on his slumped shoulders. "Still no answer?"

Ben shook his head slowly and turned around. Since Jayden had run off to be with his mother during their recent ski trip to New Zealand, Ben's milk chocolate eyes had held a haunted look, and Tessa's heart ached for him.

She'd forced herself to remain strong for both their sakes, although she feared Ben might slip back into depression if they couldn't convince Jayden to come home soon, which was becoming more unlikely with every day that passed.

Tessa lifted her hand and touched Ben's face lightly. "He'll come home. I'm sure he will."

"I don't know how you can be so confident." His eyes misted over.

"We have to trust God to work this out."

Ben inhaled slowly and nodded. "Yes, I know, but it's so hard. Especially when he won't even talk to us." His voice caught in his throat.

Tessa forced tears back as she pulled him close. The pain she was feeling was nothing compared to the despair and failure tormenting her husband. If only he'd stop blaming himself. Nobody could have foreseen what had happened. Not even Jayden's best friend, Neil, had known what Jayden and his mum had been planning.

For a long moment, Ben clung to her. Tessa didn't know what more she could say. Never in their wildest dreams had they expected Jayden to disappear.

"Maybe the lawyer will come up with something." Her voice was little more than a whisper. She wasn't convinced anything could be done, but Ben was keen to explore any possible option that might bring Jayden home.

Ben lifted his head, drawing a deep breath before nodding slowly. "I hope so. I can't handle this much longer." His voice choked again.

Tessa lifted her hand and brushed his dampened cheek with her fingers as she held his gaze. How had their holiday, the one intended to build bridges between Ben and Jayden, gone so horribly wrong? *Dear God, please help us. Please bring Jayden home.*

~

WHEN THEY ARRIVED at Preston Iken's inner city office later that morning, the receptionist showed them into a small corner office furnished with a cherry wooden desk, dark burgundy leather chairs, and shaded table lamps. She offered coffee while they waited.

They didn't have long to wait. A slightly rotund older man wearing bi-focal glasses bustled into the room before their coffee arrived. Preston Iken held out his hand. "Nice to meet you, Mr. and Mrs. Williams. Sorry I'm late."

Ben stood and shook the older man's hand. "Thanks for meeting with us, Mr. Iken."

"Please, call me Preston." He gave a dismissive wave of his hand. "Now, take a seat and tell me what I can do for you." Preston sat on the opposite side of the desk and opened a notepad.

Ben drew a deep breath. Tessa took his hand and squeezed it. Their eyes briefly met as he glanced at her for support before returning his attention to Preston. "We're hoping you can help us with a very serious matter." Ben swallowed hard before proceeding to tell Preston of his divorce from Kathryn and how she'd secretly contacted Jayden and somehow convinced him to go live with her. "She's taken him out of the country—all the way to the States, in fact, and we want him back as soon as possible." Ben's chest heaved as his chin quivered. He still couldn't believe this had happened. "Jayden belongs here. With us." Ben's voice faltered. He fought back tears as Tessa placed her arm around his shoulder.

Preston steepled his fingers, resting his chin on top. "Mmm. Parental child abduction." He leaned back in his chair and folded his arms, his expression softening as he met Ben's gaze. "First of all, I want you to know you're not alone. This kind of thing happens more often than people know. Australia has the highest rate of parental child abduction per capita in the world, not that you're probably interested in that statistic."

Ben pinched his lips and shifted restlessly in his seat. "Not really. I just want my son back."

Tessa leaned forward and glanced at Ben before turning back to Preston and giving him a polite smile. "That's an interesting fact, Mr. Iken, but what do you suggest we do about our situation?"

"Getting your son back isn't going to be easy—I'm sorry." Preston straightened in his chair and peered at Ben over the top of his glasses. "Mr. Williams, when you and your ex-wife divorced, did you get a parenting order that gave you the legal right to keep Jayden?"

Ben stiffened as he felt the colour drain from his face. "Well, no, but surely that shouldn't matter." It shouldn't matter, but somehow it did. He closed his eyes and wished this was all just a cruel dream and that he'd wake up any second and discover none of it was true. Jayden hadn't run away with Kathryn. He was alive and well and still at home. But when Ben opened his eyes, Preston's gaze was fixed on him. It wasn't a dream. It was a nightmare. Ben held Preston's gaze, even though he just wanted to crawl into a hole and hide. How could he have been so stupid?

He drew a slow breath and continued in a carefully measured, monotone voice. "Kathryn didn't want Jayden when she left. She walked out and left him with me, and I've been taking care of him ever since." He blinked back tears. "His school's here. All his friends are here. Australia's the only place Jayden's ever lived." His voice grew louder as anger over what Kathryn had done welled up within him. "She shouldn't be able to waltz in and disrupt his life like this." Ben sat forward. He was getting stirred up, but he didn't care. What Kathryn had done was wrong. Totally, one hundred percent, wrong.

Tessa placed her arm around his shoulders. He shrugged it off.

Preston scratched his chin and adjusted his thinly framed glasses. "That's what you think. And on the grounds of common sense, I agree with you; but the law says differently, I'm sorry." He leaned forward, his expression growing serious. "Since you don't have a parenting order in place for your son, there's not much preventing your ex-wife from taking him out of the country, even against your will."

Ben jolted in his seat. "You're kidding, right?"

Preston shook his head and pinched his lips. "Sadly, I'm not."

"Doesn't the fact that Jayden's a minor make any difference?" Tessa asked.

"I'm afraid not." Preston glanced at her as he removed his glasses.

Ben drew his eyebrows together. "Are you saying there's nothing we can do to get Jayden back?"

"That's not what I meant." Preston paused, running a hand over his balding head. "The Hague Convention provides a procedure for attempting to have a child returned in cases like this, but it's never easy, and unfortunately the success rate isn't great, especially when court orders aren't in place." He crossed his arms and rested his elbows on the table, his expression changing to one of reassurance. "We'll do whatever we can, but it's a complicated matter we're dealing with. Give me a few days to look into it, and then we can meet again to decide where we go to from here."

Preston continued speaking, but all Ben could hear was a sickening whirring in his head. Jayden wasn't coming home anytime soon. A lump formed in his throat, and he could barely manage a polite thank-you.

Tessa clutched his hand as they left Preston's office and entered the lift. She remained silent as he stared vacantly at the city below.

"I should have got a custody order. And I should never have trusted Kathryn."

*How could he have been so stupid?*

# CHAPTER 2

essa rolled over and reached for Ben, but instead of a warm body, her hand found a cold, empty space. She let out a sleepy sigh and opened her eyes. The neon red numbers on the clock flashed three a.m. She dragged herself out of bed, wrapped her robe around herself and tiptoed downstairs.

A flicker of light in the outdoor work area Ben had claimed for his home office caught her attention as she passed through the living room. After filling two glasses with water, she slid the door open with her foot and padded across the grass, still wet from the rain the day before. The full moon, half shrouded in wispy clouds, cast a ghostly silver glow over the entire back-yard. Tessa couldn't help but think that somewhere, halfway across the world, Jayden might also gaze at that same moon.

She draped her arm gently across Ben's hunched shoulders as she stood beside him. "Any success?" She knew the answer already, but still, she had to ask.

Ben shook his head. "No, but he's seeing my messages on Facebook." He let out a frustrated sigh and rubbed the back of his neck. "He's ignoring me on purpose."

She leaned over the back of Ben's chair and wrapped her arms around him. "It might not be Jayden's doing. Maybe Kathryn's telling him not to answer."

Ben's body stiffened. "He'd reply if he wanted to. He messaged Kathryn for months behind our backs." His breathing quickened. "I've a good mind to go over there and drag him home myself."

Tessa inhaled slowly. How many times had they had this conversation? She unwrapped her arms and perched on the edge of Ben's desk, facing him. "And what would that achieve? If you went over and dragged him back, do you think he'd stay?"

Ben shrugged before turning his attention back to the computer screen.

"We need to trust God to bring Jayden home when he's ready. Besides, we have a lawyer working on it as well."

Ben's gaze didn't shift from the screen. "Preston's been working on it for two weeks and hasn't done a thing."

Tessa crossed her arms and studied her husband. She hated what this was doing to him. There were so many 'if-only's', but the reality was that Jayden had been unhappy at home for whatever reason, and had been taken in by Kathryn's promises of a better life in America. They both believed that the life Kathryn could offer Jayden would be shallow and meaningless, but how long it would take Jayden to realise that for himself was unknown. They just had to keep praying and trusting God would work in Jayden's heart, and that one day, hopefully not too far away, he'd decide to return of his own accord. But Ben wanted to confront Jayden and force him to come back. Like that was going to work. In fact, Tessa feared it might drive him further away.

"We have to keep trusting God. He can bring Jayden home faster than you, or I, or Preston could ever do. We've been praying for Jayden for a long time, and although it doesn't seem likely right now, I believe God's heard and will answer each one of those prayers. One day Jayden will wake up to himself and choose to come back of his own accord. I know it's not easy, but we have to leave Jayden in God's hands. He wants the best for him just as much as we do. We have to trust God together." She held her hand out.

Ben slowly broke his gaze from the computer screen, took Tessa's hand in his and squeezed it. "I'm sorry. You're right. I just feel so helpless." His voice caught in his throat.

Tessa stood and eased herself onto Ben's lap. She wrapped her arms around his shoulders, pulling him close. "It'll be okay, you'll see." As she rested her head on his and prayed quietly for Jayden, tears streamed down her cheeks, dampening Ben's hair.

"Come on, let's go back to bed."

"Give me a minute, then I'll come up."

As she met Ben's gaze, her heart ached for him. He wouldn't be coming back to bed anytime soon, and there was little she could do about it. She leaned down and kissed him gently before pulling back and looking deeply into his eyes. "We'll get through this, Ben. I know we will."

He smiled weakly and nodded as she slipped off his lap.

. . .

TESSA GLANCED at the clock as she entered the house. Too late to go back to bed, especially if Ben wasn't joining her. She'd take a shower and have a longer quiet time before going to work. Passing Jayden's bedroom, she paused and peeked inside. Everything was exactly the way he'd left it before they'd gone on the ski trip to New Zealand. She stepped inside the room and turned the CD player on. It wasn't one of her favourite CD's, but the heavy metal reminded her of him nonetheless.

Books with rugby balls for book ends lined his shelf. Scouting medals and science awards hung on the wall. A tennis trophy stood on top of the eight-drawer dresser surrounded by framed photos of their dogs, Bindy and Sparky, and one photo of the three of them taken on one of their beach trips. Tessa picked up this last photo and fought back tears. She remembered the day it was taken. Jayden hadn't wanted to come and was barely smiling; but at least they were together. Now, they were thousands of miles apart.

Pressing the photo to her chest, she breathed out slowly. Ben shouldn't be taking the full blame for Jayden leaving. *If only I'd been a better stepmother, Jayden might still be here.* Perhaps her work colleague, Harrison, was right. If she'd stayed home and gone to all of Jayden's games instead of working so hard, maybe he wouldn't have felt so neglected.

She bent her head as tears flooded her eyes. She'd been so focused on trying to keep Ben positive, she hadn't thought too much about her role in Jayden's decision to leave, but she'd failed him, no doubt about it. Gulping, she squeezed back her tears. *I'm sorry, God. I messed up with Jayden. I should have spent more time with him. Done more with him, but I didn't, and now he's gone.* She sniffed and clutched the photo tighter. *Please bring Jayden home, dear God. Please give us another chance to get it right.* Tears spilled down her face as she curled up on Jayden's bed and fell asleep with the photo pressed to her heart.

Later that day, Tessa escaped into her office and closed the door. Trying to focus on work was such a challenge, even though in some ways it helped her get through the day. No one at work knew about Jayden leaving. How could she tell Harrison of all people that her teenage stepson had run off with his mother? He'd just throw it back at her and say she shouldn't have been working. Just like he'd told his own mother.

She sighed as she opened her sandwich and clicked on her personal email account. Since Jayden had disappeared, she hadn't much interest in normal things like checking emails and staying in touch with people, but the thought had hit her while sorting some invoices that Jayden might have emailed her. Unlikely, but what if he had? She quickly scanned her inbox. Her heart fell. Nothing from Jayden. But there was one from Margaret, her friend from church, who was also Harrison's mother. Tessa bit her lip. She should have called Margaret and told her about Jayden. She of all people would have understood, having been estranged from Harrison for years. But it had been hard enough telling her parents.

She clicked on Margaret's message and began to read:

'HI TESSA,

*I'm well, and I hope you and your family are doing well, too. I hope you enjoyed your holiday—you'll have to tell me all about it.*

*Missed seeing you at Bible study again last night, so thought I'd give you an update on everyone. Sherry gave birth to twins last week. All three are doing well and should be home tomorrow. We'll also have to vote on a new group leader soon because Yvonne announced her engagement and is moving to Sydney. I know the other women have to give their recommendations too, but I personally think you'd do a wonderful job as our next leader. Your strong faith and cheerful disposition is just what we need. Remember, if you have anything you want to share or anything you want us to pray for, just let me know.*

*Your friend in Christ,*

*Margaret'*

TESSA LEANED back in her chair and stared at the screen. *Strong faith?* She wasn't so sure about that. For Ben's sake she'd stayed as positive as she could over the past few weeks, but did she really believe God would answer their prayers and bring Jayden back? Margaret would make a better leader, surely. How many years had she prayed faithfully for Harrison to let go of the past and forgive her? Never once had she given up hope, even though she would have liked God to have answered more quickly.

She began to type a response but picked up the phone instead and dialed Margaret's number. Margaret answered within three rings.

"Margaret, Tessa here. Thought I'd call instead of emailing." She swallowed the lump in her throat. "I've got some news..." As she shared about Jayden's leaving, she struggled to keep her emotions intact and fought to finish the story without breaking down completely. Maybe she should have just replied to Margaret's email.

"My poor girl, that's terrible news." Margaret's compassionate voice was almost Tessa's undoing.

Tessa gripped the receiver and forced herself to stay in control. "I know. Ben and I are devastated. Can you please pray? We'd really appreciate your support."

"Of course. I'll contact the prayer group right away."

"Thank you."

As soon as Tessa hung up, her phone rang—it was Ben. Unusual for him to call during the day. She grabbed the phone and answered. "Hey Ben, how are you doing?"

Ben let out a dejected sigh. "Just came back from meeting with Preston."

"Any progress?"

"A little. Kathryn's split with Luke Emerson, which we kind of guessed. Jayden doesn't have a visa, so he can only stay in the States for ninety days legally, but Preston thinks that doesn't mean a thing. Lots of people overstay, sometimes for years. He reckons they'll just keep moving. Maybe even disappear."

"Oh Ben." Tessa's heart plummeted. At least there was half a chance of getting Jayden back if they knew where he was, but if he and Kathryn disappeared? Tessa lowered her voice. She didn't want Harrison or any of the staff listening in. "Has Preston made contact with her?"

"Not directly, but he's got her address."

"Well, that's a start. When's he lodging the child abduction application?"

"Soon. It's just about ready, but he doesn't hold much hope." Ben's voice had a resigned ring to it.

"We need to keep strong, and keep praying." Tessa closed her eyes as she held the phone to her ear. If only she was as confident as she sounded.

"I know, but it's so hard." Ben let out a sad sigh.

"We'll get through this. I know we will." *Please let that be true, God.*

"I love you, Tess." Ben's voice caught.

Tessa squeezed back tears. "I love you too, Ben."

After hanging up, she rested her head on her folded arms and let her tears flow. Early afternoon sunshine flooded her office but her body remained cold. Despite her assurances to Ben and pleas to God, despair had begun to creep into her heart. *Would Jayden ever return?*

# CHAPTER 3

 our weeks earlier

JAYDEN'S CHEST tightened as the private jet carrying him and Kathryn circled above Miami International Airport. He peered out the window at the sprawling city below. Water and skyscrapers—not so different from the Gold Coast. Just bigger. The sky was awash with streaks of red, pink, and orange as the sun inched itself slowly above the horizon. He shielded his eyes from the sun's brilliant rays as the plane banked before commencing its descent.

"Excited?" Kathryn flashed Jayden another of her over-the-top smiles from her leather reclining chair opposite him. During the flight, which had been the coolest flight he'd ever been on, the plane being decked out like a small fancy apart-ment with leather lounges, flat screen televisions, and full surround sound, Jayden had got the feeling that his mum was trying too hard. There was something fake about her smile, as if she was trying to convince herself and him that she was happy. And she'd hugged him way too much. He was fifteen, for goodness' sake, not five.

Jayden nodded. "Yeah. It looks great." He tried to sound enthusiastic, but truth was, he didn't know whether to be excited or nervous. Was his decision to leave Dad and Tessa and start a new life with his mum in Florida a good one? She'd promised him so much, but he didn't really know her anymore. He continued gazing out the window until the plane hit the runway and began taxiing towards the terminal.

"Well, here we are, Jay!" Kathryn leaned forward and squeezed his knee as she flashed him another one of those smiles. Jayden winced at the nickname she'd given him. Neither Dad, Tessa, nor Neil had ever shortened his name. A lump formed in his throat. They'd probably be out looking for him.

"Come on Jay, grab your bag and let's get out of here." Kathryn stood and adjusted her shirt. She flicked her hair over her shoulder as Jayden pulled his lime-green and black duffle bag out of the storage shelf. Slinging the bag over his shoulder, he followed Kathryn down the stairs. She looked more like a model than a mother in her skinny jeans and tight fitting shirt.

They whizzed through Passport Control. Arriving by private jet must hold certain privileges. Kathryn led the way to a fancy looking black convertible parked near the terminal. Jayden whistled under his breath as he climbed in and clicked on his seatbelt. *Mum really has done all right for herself.*

"Like it?" Kathryn tilted her head, raising one eyebrow as she lowered the roof.

"Yeah, it's cool." Jayden turned his head and held his mother's gaze. "Is this the car you said I can learn on?"

"The very one." Kathryn smiled smugly as she brought the car to life and accelerated towards the freeway.

The faintest of smiles grew on Jayden's face. Maybe it was going to be all right after all.

"You're so quiet, Jay," Kathryn shouted as she looked over her designer sunglasses at him. The wind whipped her hair as she zipped around the slower cars.

Jayden let out a shaky laugh. "It's hard to talk over the noise." But really, he wasn't sure what to say. He'd like to know if Luke would be there when they arrived. She'd only mentioned him once the whole time they were on the plane, which was kind of strange. Last time he'd seen his mum was at that Pro-Am tournament in Brisbane. The day he'd discovered she'd left Dad for Luke Emerson, the international golfer he'd admired for years. Jayden's chest heaved at the memory. He'd been so angry that day, and he'd vowed never to see her, or Luke, again. So what was he doing sitting in a car with her now? And what would it be like living in a house with Luke Emerson? Jayden's heartbeat quickened.

He had to know if Luke would be there. Jayden swallowed hard and stared ahead, waiting until Kathryn slowed down. When she exited the freeway and entered a residential area, he cleared his throat. "I...I was just wondering who's going to be there." He pinched his fingers together as he waited for the answer.

Kathryn glanced at him as she turned into a broad tree-lined avenue. Huge mansions stretched into the distance as far as the eye could see, but the streets were empty. "No one, Jay. It's just you and me." Her voice was slightly high-pitched and wobbly.

Jayden's head shot around. "You're not with Luke anymore?"

"Didn't I tell you?" She gave a dismissive wave of her hand and lifted her chin.

Jayden let out a huge sigh of relief.

She opened her mouth as if to say something else, but instead, raised her hand to her cheek. Was she wiping tears from her eyes? He wasn't sure. She glanced at him and swallowed before she gave him another of her smiles. "We're going to have such fun together, Jay."

He drew a deep breath as he tried to control the thumping in his chest. *Surely Mum didn't just want me here because Luke's gone. She wouldn't do that, would she?* He studied her as she continued talking, a little too fast and a little too upbeat. Maybe she was just nervous.

"My place is new, and I think you'll love it, Jay. It's right on the water and we'll be able to do so many things together."

He forced a smile before turning to look out the window. The clear crystal water and sunny blue sky reminded him of Australia and his last outing to the Gold Coast with Dad and Tessa. He hadn't wanted to go, but Dad had made him. At least he'd got to go jet-skiing.

The ring of his cell phone sounded from his pocket. He pulled it out and sighed. *Dad. Again. How many times has he called?* Every time the plane had stopped to fuel up, all Dad's missed calls had popped up, but this one was live. Dad was calling right now. Jayden's pulse quickened. Should he answer? Every time he thought about the way he'd left, without an explanation and without even saying goodbye, his chest tightened. He shifted in his seat and was tempted to answer, but then the ringing stopped.

Kathryn peered over. "You know you can block his number so you don't have to be bothered with him calling."

Jayden stared at the phone for a second and then slipped it back into his pocket. He shrugged. It was too soon to block Dad's number.

Kathryn slowed the car and turned into a parking lot with a well-lit sign reading 'Biscayne Bay Luxury Homes'.

Jayden's eyebrows lifted. *Fancy. Very fancy.* He followed her to the entrance of the luxury condo.

"Well, here we are, Jay. What do you think?" She held the door open, her eyes bright and expectant.

He stepped inside. The house at New Farm was pretty cool, not that he'd ever told Dad and Tessa that, but this was sick. The water was right there, just through the glass doors. He couldn't hide the excitement in his voice as he walked towards the view. "It's amazing!"

"And there's more. Let me show you your room." She tossed her purse onto the glossy kitchen counter and ran upstairs ahead of him. "Come on."

He followed her, taking the steps two at a time. His bedroom was twice as large as his room back home, and had sliding glass doors opening onto a balcony overlooking the bay. Miami's downtown skyline filled the horizon to the left. The view made Jayden's jaw drop. He dragged himself away and took in the rest of his room. A new computer sat on a glossy white desk; an HD television with surround sound speakers had been fitted onto the wall at the foot of his bed, a collection of CDs was stacked beside his bed and posters of some of his favourite rock bands hung in frames on the wall. But his eyes popped at the shiny, new, Gibson guitar sitting on a stand beside his bed.

He dropped his duffle bag onto the floor and picked the guitar up, caressing its smooth finish and running his hands lightly across the strings. He'd always dreamed of owning a guitar like this but had never expected to get one.

"Do you like it?"

He lifted his head. Kathryn stood in the doorway. Her eyes glowed and she was fidgeting with her hands. He hesitated, but then put the guitar down and stepped towards her.

"I love it. I really do." He lifted his gaze to meet hers. "Thank you. Mum."

"You're welcome." Her eyes glistened as her face expanded into a warm smile. She took Jayden's hands. "I'm so glad you like it." She led him to the balcony and leaned on the railing, looking out at the expansive bay. "There's so much to do here. You can go swimming or jet-skiing whenever you like. Or bike riding or roller blading, whatever you want." She turned to face him. "You're going to have a great time here, I just know it." He tilted his head. Her eyes were so bright, and bluer than he remembered, almost too blue. *Maybe she's done something to them.* Before he knew it, tears welled in her eyes and she was drawing him into a big hug. *Here we go again.* He stood with his arms by his side for a moment, but he inhaled slowly and finally lifted them and returned her hug. He owed her that at least for all she'd done for him. *She'd better not expect it all the time, though.*

When she finally let him go, she wiped her face with a tissue and ran her finger under her eye. Black stuff had run onto her cheeks, but she smeared it and made it worse. "I'll just go and freshen up and then we can hang out for a while."

As soon as she left, Jayden flopped backwards onto his bed, placing his hands behind his head. He stared up at the ceiling and smiled. If all he had to do was put up with an emotional mother to have all this luxury right at his fingertips, maybe he could forget all about Brisbane and Dad and Tessa.

# CHAPTER 4

*E*arly the next morning, Jayden lifted his head slowly from his pillow and rubbed sleep from his eyes. His head spun. Where was he? Crazy dreams about ski slopes, airplanes, and Mum and Dad fighting over him confused his thinking. Jerking up in bed, he flicked on the lamp and then flopped back on his pillow. That's right. He was in his new bedroom at Mum's condo, in Miami, Florida. And it was Sunday.

He lay there for a few moments gathering his thoughts. If he was at home, Dad and Tessa would be making him go to church. Mum probably didn't go anymore, so that meant he could spend the day exploring.

Throwing off the covers, Jayden jumped out of bed and opened the shutters. Below, the crystal clear water of the bay shimmered in the early morning sunshine. A number of speed boats were heading out to deeper waters, presumably to fish, leaving a spray of white water behind them, and closer in to shore, stand-up paddle boarders bobbed up and down in the gentle waves as they moved along the shoreline. Early morning joggers and cyclists shared the pathway that weaved along the water's edge. The Brisbane River had nothing on this, and Jayden couldn't wait to get down there.

He turned from the window and padded down the darkened hallway before knocking tentatively on his mum's door. No response. He knocked again, this time a little louder. She must still be asleep. He'd almost given up when she called out.

"Come in, Jay." She sounded sleepy. He must have woken her.

Jayden drew a breath and pushed the door ajar. She was still in bed, struggling to sit up. Her eyes still had black smudges under them, and her hair, normally so shiny and straight, was disheveled and messy.

"Good morning, Jay." She yawned, rubbing her eyes, making the black even more pronounced. She adjusted her pillows. "Awake already? I didn't think you'd be such an early riser, being a teenager and all."

He stepped a little closer and leaned on the door. "I'm not normally. Must be jet lag."

"If you're not going back to bed you could check out the beach and use the jet ski. I'll come down in a while. I need to get some more beauty sleep." She yawned again. "Get yourself some breakfast. There's plenty of food in the pantry." She slid back down and curled up, pulling the sheet around her before giving him a sleepy smile.

"Okay." Jayden raised an eyebrow. Dad would never let him go out like that on his own. And Dad and Tessa were usually up before him. Most mornings they'd eat breakfast together, not that he really liked sitting at the table with them, but eating on his own? On the first morning? Jayden backed out of the room and shut the door. This was definitely different.

He wandered down to the kitchen and opened the fridge. His eyes popped. Mum had gone overboard. Did she think he hadn't eaten for a year or something? Piles of pre-cooked meals, bottles of soda, juice and milk filled every space. Next Jayden opened the pantry. It overflowed with cookies of all shapes and sizes, packets of potato chips, and six different cereals. All unopened.

He filled his bowl with Chocolate Cheerios before plonking onto the couch and switching on the television. With no-one around to tell him off, he put his feet on the coffee table.

As he ate, Jayden flicked through the channels, but his eyelids drooped. Maybe the exploration could wait—a little more sleep wouldn't hurt. As he climbed back into his bed a few minutes later, he pulled out his phone and flipped through the messages. One text message from Neil and several from Dad. His heart grew heavy. The messages from Dad all said the same thing. He and Tessa wanted to know if he was safe. They loved him and were praying for him to come home. They wanted to know why he'd left. Bindy and Sparky missed him too. Jayden fought back tears as he scrolled through the messages. He'd like to respond, but what would he say? *Sorry?* That sounded lame, and it certainly wouldn't make up for the hurt he'd caused. He sighed and slipped the phone under his pillow. He'd sleep on it. Tears pricked his eyes as images of Dad and Tessa and Bindy and Sparky drifted through his mind. Maybe he could stay with Mum for just a few days and then go home. But how could he do that? She'd been looking forward to him coming, and had bought all those things... Not only his head, but his heart, hurt. Squeezing his eyes shut, Jayden buried his face in his pillow and forced all those thoughts from his head.

A little while later, he woke to sunlight streaming in through the glass doors. The condo was completely quiet— Mum must still be sleeping. He took a shower and put on the wet-suit Mum had given him the night before and strolled down to the jetty to check out the jet skis. He couldn't believe his own mother had a private jetty, let alone two jet skis and a fancy boat. Dad had a small sailboat, but nothing like this.

The water of Biscayne Bay was warm and blue as he gunned the powerful engine of the burnt orange jet ski and sped away from the wooden jetty. Being in the water, with the sun shining down on him, made him forget about the tears he'd shed earlier. As the wind whipped his hair and brushed his face, he cast any lingering doubts aside. Zooming across the water, he had not a care in the world.

IT WAS mid-afternoon when Kathryn sauntered down to the beach in plaid shorts and a wide-brimmed straw hat. Jay was about fifty feet away on the jet ski. She cupped her hand around her mouth and called out. He waved and yelled something back, but she couldn't hear. He certainly looked like he was having fun. She stood and watched a few moments longer before boarding the boat moored to the jetty. Although not as impressive as Luke's boat, it still had a decent-sized cabin containing a kitchen, a bed which doubled as a lounge, and a small sitting area. Kathryn poured a glass of wine and eased herself onto the lounge. Exhaling contentedly, she stretched out her long legs and stared out over the water, a smile growing on her face each time Jay zoomed past.

It was good having him here. Ever since Luke Emerson had dumped her for that younger woman, she'd been lonely. Even the wives and girlfriends of Luke's fellow golfers had deserted her, and now there were no friends to go shopping with or even to drop in on for a cup of tea, *or something stronger.* Spending so much time on her own was driving her crazy. But then she got the idea of luring Jay to come live with her. Jay wasn't happy with Ben and that new wife of his, so he'd told her, so it hadn't been that difficult to convince him to come.

Kathryn smiled to herself as she refilled her wine glass. Now Jay was here, she wouldn't have to worry about going to the beach on her own, nor would she have to spend day after day by herself in the condo she'd bought with the settlement money she'd been entitled to after being Luke Emerson's partner for the past three years. Now Jay was here, she wouldn't let him go. Ben could try as much as he liked to get him back, but good luck to him. Miami Beach, Florida, or Brisbane, Queensland? She knew which one she'd choose, and Jay would too once he got to know it. So many things for him to do. She let out a happy sigh as Jay zoomed past again. *He'll never want to go back.*

As Kathryn sipped her wine, thoughts of Luke flitted through her mind. She stared at the wine glass as she twirled the thin stem slowly between her fingers. Why had she pressured him to marry her? If only she'd been happy to remain as his girlfriend, they'd probably still be together. She could still see his sparkling eyes and his tanned, toned body. They'd been so happy, or so she'd thought. Tears spilled down her face. Now it was all over. Kathryn swallowed the sobs collecting at the base of her throat and sculled the last of her wine.

"Is everything okay, Mum?"

Kathryn blinked and turned towards the cabin door. Jay, lean and trim in his wet glistening suit, stood looking at her. She met his gaze and sucked in a breath. She hadn't really noticed how much like Ben he looked. They had the same eyes. Eyes that could melt a girl's heart in an instant. How many hearts would Jay break?

"Mum?"

"Oh, yes." She straightened, quickly wiping her face as she set her glass aside. "Just thinking about things." She held her hand out to him. "Have fun?"

"Yeah, it was awesome."

She smiled. "You must be famished. Let me fix something to eat."

"Thanks." Jay walked around the cabin, exploring all the hidden spaces and wood paneled cabinets. "Can we take it out?"

Kathryn raised her eyebrows. "The boat?" She opened the mini refrigerator and took out a platter of cold cut sandwiches and a pack of strawberry Jell-O cups.

Jay nodded as he stuffed a sandwich into his mouth.

"Not unless you know how to sail it."

His brows knitted as he swallowed his mouthful. "So, you have a boat like this, but you can't sail?"

She let out a small chuckle and waved dismissively. "It's good for entertaining."

"Right." Jay took another sandwich and woofed it down. "Dad was teaching me to sail, but I've never been out in a boat as big as this."

"I'll get you some lessons if you like, and then you can take me sailing." She held out her hand. "Come and sit beside me, Jay."

Jay complied and took a seat next to her. She poured a glass of crisp ginger ale for him, then picked up her glass of wine and held it up for a toast. "To us."

He guffawed and almost spilled his drink.

"Oh, come on, Jay. We need to celebrate being together again." Kathryn held her glass up once more and clinked it against his. "To us."

"To us." Jay's expression grew serious as he repeated the words dutifully before taking a sip.

"I was thinking we could go to Miami Beach this afternoon. What do you say?" She placed her hand lightly on his shoulder.

He shrugged. "Sounds good. As long as I can swim."

"Yes, you can swim as much as you want. And then maybe we can have dinner out." She twirled his hair in her fingers. "You need to make the most of this week, because next week you start school."

Jay's mouth fell open. "School?"

"Yes. You can't fall behind on your schooling just because you're living here." Kathryn rested her elbow on the back of the seat.

He folded his arms and humphed. "I'd rather not go. It'll be a lot different to what I'm used to."

"Don't look so worried." Kathryn continued twirling his hair, but he shrugged her hand away. She placed her arm lightly around his shoulder and pulled him closer. His body tensed, but this time he didn't pull away. "I've checked all the schools in the area and chosen the best one for you. You'll meet a lot of new friends your age and the teachers will make sure you fit right in. I'm sure a few things will be different, but it'll be fun. You'll do just fine." She flashed him a reassuring smile, but the hard line set on his mouth suggested she'd failed to convince him.

# CHAPTER 5

*A*ll through the week, Jayden tried to get out of going to school, but Kathryn wouldn't hear of it. She bought him an abundance of new supplies and clothes to make sure he'd be ready to start. The following Monday morning, she drove him to the sprawling Biscayne Bay campus of Miranda High.

Jayden sat in the passenger seat in stony silence, staring straight ahead. When she pulled into a parking spot in front of the school, he didn't move. On his right, swarms of students, parents, and teachers milled around in the open area between the parking lot and the school buildings. Miranda High was much larger than his school back home. When she'd told him he didn't have to wear a uniform, he hadn't believed her, but she was right. None of the students wore uniforms; instead they were dressed in jeans, knee-length shorts, and whatever else it seemed they wanted to wear.

A glossy red Mustang purred to a stop beside their car.

Jayden turned his head. A boy not much older than himself jumped out of the driver's seat and started up the walkway.

"When can you teach me to drive?" Jayden asked without turning his head back.

Mum laughed nervously.

Jayden spun his head around, drawing his eyebrows together. "What's funny about that? You promised."

She let out a shaky sigh, the color draining from her face. "I might have made a teeny mistake."

"What do you mean?" He glared at her.

She drew a slow breath and reached her hand out, but he leaned further away.

"Come on, Jay. Give me a break. I thought you could get your Learner's, but seems you can't since you're not a resident yet."

He cast her a veiled glance and slumped in his seat. "You promised."

"I know, and I'm sorry. Please forgive me. I really didn't know."

Jayden shook his head, pursing his lips. How could she not know? She shouldn't have made promises she couldn't keep. The dreams he'd had of driving down the freeway in a black convertible with the top down and the wind whipping his hair were now dashed. *I may as well go home.* That way he wouldn't have to start at this horrible school. He slumped further in his seat.

"Come on, Jay. We can talk more later, but now you've got to get out of the car and go to school." She reached out and touched his face with the back of her hand.

He pushed it away and glared at her again. "Fine." He opened the door and climbed out, slamming it behind him.

"I'll pick you up this afternoon." Her voice trailed off as he strode towards the school building with his head down.

Jayden's eyes filled with angry tears and he breathed heavily. As soon as he was sure his mother couldn't see him, he brushed his eyes with the back of his hand and slowed down. He had to get a grip on himself before classes started. Bad enough to be the new guy—no way could he let anyone see he'd been crying.

Keeping his eyes lowered, he joined the throng of students moving towards the entrance. A few walked alone, but most talked and laughed with one or more friends. His shoulders sagged under the weight of his military-style canvas messenger bag that carried one too many notepads and textbooks.

As he walked down the brightly-lit hallways, an empty feeling grew in the pit of his stomach. His mouth was dry and his chest tight. The other students all looked like they belonged. He, on the other hand, felt very much out of place and wished Neil could be here with him. Or that he was back at his old school.

He pulled the day's schedule out of his messenger bag. Compared to how simple and organized things had been at his old school, this was really confusing. The day was divided into four periods—first, second, third, and fourth. Two classes in each period with a lunch break between the second and third. Time for gym and other sports activities like football and basketball were also scheduled. No mention of a rugby, tennis, or rowing team. *Mum had better not have signed me up for a sport I don't know, like Gridiron.*

"Neat shoes." Jayden looked up to see who owned the husky voice. In front of him stood the owner of the red Mustang. Dressed in a team jacket and with a shock of blonde hair, the boy had a basketball tucked under his arm, and stood a head taller than Jayden.

"Thanks." Jayden glanced down at his gold and black Nike sneakers and tried to think of something else to say. He lifted his head. "I saw your car out there. It's nice. Is it yours?"

"Yep. Bought it last year." The boy held out his hand. "I'm Keith, by the way. You must be new. Haven't seen you before."

"Yeah, I'm Jayden, and this is my first day." Jayden shook Keith's hand. "I'm a bit confused by the schedule."

"I can help. We might be in the same classes." Keith took the paper and studied it, then shook his head and shrugged. "Nope. You're in tenth grade. I'm in twelfth. Looks like your first class is Biology, though. Maybe we can find a teacher around here who can help you."

"Hey, Keith." A tall brunette in a cheerleader outfit bounced up beside him and linked her arm into Keith's.

"Hey, Lori." Keith's face lit up as Lori kissed his cheek.

She tilted her head and looked Jayden's way. "Who's this?"

"Jayden. He's new."

If only the floor would open up and swallow him. "Hi." Jayden gulped. He wasn't used to talking with girls. Well, not girls that looked like Lori.

"Why are you talking like that?" Lori asked.

"Like what?"

Lori screwed up her nose and tapped her chin with a finger. "I don't know. You sound kind of nasally. Oh, wait...you must be British."

"No, I'm from Australia." Jayden jerked his head up. How could she even think he was British?

Lori laughed. "My bad. I'm always getting those two mixed up. But Australia's a totally cool place. My parents and I went to Sydney for vacation last year, and we loved it. I bet you're a bit homesick being so far away, but Florida's pretty cool too. You'll get used to it after a while."

Just then the bell rang and students started disappearing into the various classrooms. "Oh, well, we better get going," Keith said. "It was nice meeting you, Jayden. Maybe we can meet up at lunch."

"Later." Lori waved as she tucked her arm tighter into Keith's.

Jayden gazed longingly after them as they moved off down the hall together, Keith spinning the basketball on his index finger and Lori hanging off his arm. He wouldn't admit it to anyone, but he was feeling homesick. The week he'd spent with Mum had been fun, but he was missing his friends, especially Neil. And just that morning, Dad had called again and he'd been tempted to pick up, but Mum had been nearby, and he just couldn't bring himself to do it. Dad seemed to be getting more agitated though. How many Facebook messages and emails had he sent? Jayden had lost count. He'd have to reply soon, but what would he say?

Sighing heavily, Jayden looked for someone to give him directions. He selected a man dressed in a suit and asked him where the tenth grade Biology class was. The man pointed him in the right direction, and in a few minutes Jayden arrived outside a door that read 'Mr. Miller - Biology, Sophomore Hall'. Pausing a moment, Jayden took a deep breath to steady himself before slipping inside the room. The other students were already in place and Mr. Miller had just started going over preliminaries.

Everyone looked up. Once again, Jayden wished the floor would open up. "Sorry I'm late." He was very aware of his accent now Lori had commented on it.

"That's fine." Mr. Miller had a deep voice and boomed every word. "You must be Jayden. Come on in. Put your bag over there and take the empty seat in the third row."

"Thanks." Jayden nodded and did as he was told. He pulled out his textbook for that class and took his seat. It was going to be a long day.


AT LUNCH, Jayden looked around for Keith and eventually spotted him sitting at a table with Lori and a group of other boys and girls who all seemed to be basketball players or cheerleaders. All in twelfth grade. Maybe he should sit with someone in his own grade. He was about to walk away when Keith stood and waved him over.

"This is Jayden, everyone." Keith introduced him to the others.

"He's from Australia." Lori sounded as if she was announcing a popular rock star.

Keith pulled Jayden closer until his mouth was near Jayden's ear. "Sophomores don't normally sit with seniors, but since it's your first day, you can sit with us. But you'll need to sit with your own crew tomorrow. Got it?"

Jayden nodded. He should have just sat by himself.

"Do you play?" a boy with cropped black hair and a gold chain around his neck asked.

"Play what?"

The boy gave him a strange look as if he was stupid. "Basketball, of course."

Jayden shook his head. "I play rugby."

"You're not in Aussie anymore, dude." Keith said.

"What's rugby?" Lori leaned forward.

"It's supposed to be some type of football, but they play it all wrong," the boy with the dark cropped hair said.

The boy attempted to explain the game to Lori, but got it all wrong. Jayden had a mind to tell the boy he didn't know what he was talking about, but kept his mouth shut. No use getting into an argument on his first day, especially with a senior.

Jayden's phone rang. His shoulders slumped. *Not Dad again.* He pulled it from his pocket and the corners of his mouth quirked up. *Not Dad. Neil.*

"Gotta take this, sorry." He stood and left the table. He quickly found the bathroom and locked himself into a stall.

"Jayden," Neil said as his blurry face came into view on Jayden's phone screen. "How are you doing?"

Tears stung Jayden's eyes. He quickly wiped them away. "Not bad. What about you?"

"Not bad, either. It's four in the morning and I should be sleeping. Mum doesn't know I'm awake so I can't talk too loud. What are you doing?"

"I'm at school." Jayden lowered his voice as well.

"Oh." Neil was quiet for a few moments. "What's it like?"

"I don't know anyone. It's all different, and so far I don't like it."

CHAPTER 5 | 37

"When are you coming back home?"

Jayden was silent. He shrugged. "I don't know."

"Come back soon. I really miss you, Jayden. It's not the same without you here."

The bell rang. "I have to go, Neil. Sorry."

"No problem, I'll call back later." Neil pulled one of his funny faces until the screen went blank.

Jayden closed his eyes and squeezed back the tears that were threatening to fall. He was fifteen, for goodness' sake. He shouldn't be crying. What would Keith and the others think if they saw him? But the pain in his heart was heavy, and seeing Neil just made it worse. Maybe he should go home.

The second warning bell sounded. Wiping his face with his sleeve, he slipped his phone into his pocket before heading back to class.

The rest of the day passed slowly, as did the rest of the week. After surviving his first five days at Miranda High, Jayden was more than happy to see the weekend. He slept two extra hours on Saturday morning before shuffling into the kitchen to get something to eat. Mum was already awake and sitting at the counter with a cup of hot tea. She looked up from the laptop open in front of her and gave him one of her bright smiles.

"Any plans for today?" Jayden pulled a box of cereal out of the cupboard and sat at the breakfast bar. If there weren't any, he'd take the jet ski out again since Mum hadn't made any plans for the sailing lessons—nor the driving lessons. Had she forgotten?

Mum's eyes were on him. "What would you like to do?" She

put her mug of tea down and leaned closer. "Is everything okay, Jay?"

Jayden glanced up. "Yeah, everything's fine." He let out a heavy sigh as he placed a spoonful of cereal into his mouth. Milk dripped down his chin, and he wiped it with his hand. "So, no special plans for the weekend?" Jayden continued with his original question.

"Not really. We could go to the movies tomorrow, but right now, I'm just checking into a few things."

"Like what?" He tilted his head.

She shrugged and turned the screen away from him. "Nothing important."

Jayden narrowed his eyes. What was she working on? And why did he get the feeling something was wrong?

"Go and have some fun, Jay. We'll go to the movies tomorrow."

"I'll take the jet ski out again." Jayden placed his empty bowl into the dishwasher and left the kitchen.

# CHAPTER 6

*A* soft knock sounded on the door of Ben's office in downtown Brisbane. Although his was a corner office, half enclosed in glass windows with a striking view of the Brisbane River and the Story Bridge, these days he rarely noticed it. Straightening in his leather chair, Ben glanced at the clock. Where had the afternoon gone? He let out a deep sigh and saved his work before turning to the door.

"Come in." Even to him, his voice sounded tired and strained.

Walton stuck his head inside the door. "I'm calling it a day, mate. You should too."

Ben rubbed the back of his neck and met Walton's gaze. "I've still got a few numbers to crunch, Walt. Think I'll be working late again."

"This is the fifth straight day you've worked overtime. You should go home." Walton's expression grew serious. "Tessa needs you."

Ben leaned back in his chair and looked out the window. The sky, awash with pinks and oranges, was darkening quickly. Yes, he should go home. He didn't really need to be at work, but being at home made him think about Jayden. And the more he thought about Jayden, the more depressed he became. The house was so quiet these days. As much as he hated Jayden's loud music, what he'd give now to hear it when he arrived home. To hear Jayden laughing in the backyard with the dogs, even to see his mess scattered through the house. He let out another deep sigh as he swivelled around slowly to face Walton.

"Yes, I know. I'll go shortly."

Walton narrowed his eyes. "Make sure you do. I know what you're like. See you Monday." He gave a short nod and left the room.

As Walton's footsteps receded, Ben slumped onto his desk, placing his head on his crossed forearms. A wave of numbing sadness washed over him. He'd done everything wrong. Jayden's decision to leave was totally his fault, and he was drowning under the weight of guilt and despair. He swallowed hard as the pain in his heart grew heavier. *God, please bring Jayden back. I'm sorry for everything. I can't handle this much longer.*

Ben's phone rang. He drew in a deep breath and raised his head. It would be Tessa.

"Where are you, Ben? I've cooked dinner and I've been waiting for almost an hour."

He closed his eyes and rubbed the bridge of his nose. He needed to go home. To Tessa. "I'm sorry, Tess, I'll come now."

As he stood, Ben glanced out the window. On the street

below, a man and a boy of about ten years old were leaving a sweet shop. As they walked hand in hand down the sidewalk to their car, tears pricked Ben's eyes. If only he could wind the clock back.

On his way home, he stopped at a florist and bought a bunch of flowers. Just as well, because when he arrived home, Tessa stood in the doorway with her arms folded and her lips pinched.

He grimaced. He hated seeing her upset. And it was all his fault. He stepped out of the car and moved towards her, flowers in hand. "Tess, I'm so sorry." Tears pricked his eyes as her expression softened and she held out her arms and pulled him towards her.

"It's okay. Just don't shut me out. Please?" She lifted her hand and slipped it behind his neck, drawing his face closer to hers. Her eyes, only inches from his, reflected the pain he was feeling. "We'll get through this. I know we will."

He squeezed back his tears as he took her face gently in his hands. "I hope so." He lowered his mouth and kissed her slowly and tenderly. "I love you." His voice was little more than a trembling whisper as his heart beat with love for his beautiful wife.

AFTER DINNER, Tessa suggested they take the dogs for a walk. To her surprise, Ben agreed. But when Sunday morning came and he said he didn't feel like going to church, her new found hope that he was pulling himself out of his depression slipped away.

She sat down on the bed and leaned over him, propping herself on one elbow as she ran her fingers playfully along his jaw. "Won't you come with me? Please?"

"Not today." Ben pushed himself up on the pillows. Dark circles hung under his eyes. "I'm sorry, but I just don't feel like going." He drew in a slow breath. "I can't face everyone again."

"Oh Ben. No-one's judging."

"That's what you think."

"If they are, that's their problem. They just care, that's all."

He raised a brow. "Really? If they cared, why do I feel we're being stared at all the time?"

Tessa exhaled slowly. "They're not staring. Most people don't even know what's happened. As far as they're concerned, Jayden's just gone to live with his mother."

Ben shook his head. "I still feel I'm being judged." He stroked her face and looked into her eyes. "I'm not losing my faith, if that's what you're thinking. And I'm not questioning God. Well... maybe a little. But I just can't face all those people at the moment with their happy families."

With a heavy heart, Tessa sighed as she rested her head against his chest and gently caressed his arm. *If only he'd let his walls down and allow people to minister to him rather than thinking they were judging him.* After a short while, she tilted her head. "It's okay. I'll go on my own."


WHEN TESSA RETURNED from church a few hours later, Ben was in the kitchen making sandwiches. She set her purse and Bible down on a nearby chair and draped her arm across his shoulder as she kissed him lightly on the cheek. "Feeling better, sweetie?" She squeezed his shoulder, and her heart warmed when he turned and kissed her.

"A little." His voice was still tinged with sadness, but any improvement was better than none.

She filled two glasses with ice and grabbed a jug of juice from the fridge. "The sandwiches look great."

The corners of Ben's mouth lifted slightly. "Thought I'd do something useful while you were out."

"Thank you." She smiled warmly at him before carrying the glasses to the outdoor table.

"This is nice. We need to do it more often."

Ben lifted his face and squeezed her hand. The dark circles still sat under his eyes, and she didn't like the deep furrow that had formed on his forehead. Her heart ached for him as she held his gaze. *God, only You can heal broken hearts. Please heal Ben's.*

"It still doesn't feel right without Jayden here." Ben turned his head away, fixing his gaze on Jayden's bike sitting in the rack to the side of the deck.

She took his hand. "I know, but we can't change what's happened."

As Ben turned to face her, his eyes glistened. "If only I'd done things differently."

"Stop blaming yourself, Ben. It's not helping. We have to be strong together, and in God, and we'll get through it."

"I don't know how to get through it, that's the problem. It's so easy to say we have to trust God," he paused, "but this cloud's hovering over me, and it doesn't want to lift, regardless of what I do."

She wrapped her arms around his shoulder. "You poor

thing. I can't even begin to imagine how you're feeling." She leaned up and kissed his cheek and wiped away the tears rolling down his cheek with her fingers. "Pastor Fraser referred to a verse this morning which spoke to my heart. It was Matthew 11, verse 29." She straightened a little. "You know the verse, Ben. 'Take my yoke upon you and learn from me, for I am gentle and humble in heart, and you will find rest for your souls.'" She squeezed his hand. "That's what we need. Rest for our souls. We need to pray more, and read the Bible together like we did before all this happened. Let God transform our hearts and our minds. He can give us peace in our hearts in the midst of all this."

Ben drew in a slow breath. "I don't know if it's as simple as that. I agree we should pray more, and read the Word more. But you know I'm prone to depression, and I think it's got me again."

Tears pricked Tessa's eyes. Hearing Ben admit this was unexpected, but he was right. He needed help, professional help, and it was wrong of her to simplify the solution. It was so easy for Christians, including herself, who'd never suffered from depression, to gloss over its effects and suggest the person should just be more spiritual.

"Maybe you should see your doctor?"

"Yes, I think so."

She met his gaze and a moment of silence passed between them. "Can I pray?"

Ben nodded, giving her a wistful smile.

She placed her arm on his shoulder and held his hand. "Dear Heavenly Father, You know our hearts are breaking, and we feel at such a loss. Lord God, I pray that You'll help us to get through this, and that You'll wrap Ben in Your loving arms and give him peace. Please give the doctor wisdom to know how to treat him, and please be with Jayden. Look after him, Lord God, and please bring him back to us soon. Thank You for Your love. You only want the best for us, Lord, and we're sorry for not trusting You enough, and for carrying the blame for what's happened when we know we can't change it. Lord, please forgive us and take us by the hand as we continue on this journey that's been threatening to tear us apart. In Jesus' name, Amen."

"Amen." Ben swiped tears from his eyes as he lifted his head. "Thank you."

Tessa smiled broadly at him. "We'll get through this, and we'll come out the other side as better people. I know we will."

DR. STEWART HAD BEEN Ben's personal physician for ten years. An even-tempered elderly man with a steady heart, he held genuine concern for his patients. After giving Ben a physical exam the next day, he said there was nothing physically wrong with him.

Ben knew that.

Dr. Stewart placed Ben's medical folder on his desk, leaned back in his swivel chair and folded his arms. "But something's bothering you."

Ben lowered his head and fidgeted with his hands. Why was it so hard to talk about it? Easier just to pretend nothing was wrong, but could he really continue living with this cloud hovering over him, day in and day out? Tessa's prayer had touched his heart, and he wished it was just as simple as she'd initially suggested. Why couldn't God just lift the cloud from him? How often in the past had he heard that Christians shouldn't suffer from depression? But he knew better than to question God. Depression was a mental illness, and as horrible as it sounded, it was real, and he needed treatment.

He drew a breath and lifted his head, holding the doctor's gaze for several seconds. "I think my depression's back."

Dr. Stewart tapped his chin. "Mmm. I think you might be right. Would you like to talk about it?" He glanced at the clock. "I've got a few minutes."

Ben ran his hand through his hair. How could he summarise what had happened and how he was feeling in a couple of minutes? He let out a heavy sigh. "There's really not much to say. Jayden, my son, has chosen to live with his mother in America, and I'm feeling like I failed him. I haven't been eating or sleeping, and my wife's concerned about me, and I'm just feeling down all the time." He shrugged. "I guess that's it in a nutshell."

Dr. Stewart's eyes softened. "I'm so sorry to hear that, Ben. It must be a difficult time for both you and your wife, so I can certainly understand why your depression's returned. Let me write you a script, and I think you should get some more counselling." He lifted his face. "How did you find that counsellor I referred you to last time?"

Ben let out a small chuckle. "How long have you got?"

Dr. Stewart cocked his head, drawing his brows together as he wrote out the script. "A few seconds, why?"

"Let's just say it was an interesting experience." Ben's

expression grew serious. "She had an accident recently, and seems she might be paralysed for life."

Dr. Stewart looked up from his writing. "That's not good to hear. Poor girl."

"Yes, it turned out she's my wife's best friend, so no, it's not good."

"You've got a lot going on. Here, take this, and come back in two weeks. In the meantime, here's a referral to a different counsellor who's a specialist with mental health issues. He'll be able to help you." Dr. Stewart stood and held out his hand. "Good luck, Ben. I'll look forward to seeing you again soon."

AFTER LEAVING the doctor's office, Ben sat in his car in the parking lot for a few minutes before heading back to work. He was tired of forcing a smile on his face and pretending everything was fine. The medication would help, but he needed to speak with Jayden, find out if he was truly happier with Kathryn than with him and Tess. Having no contact at all was killing him. *Am I that bad a father?* Ben placed his arms on the steering wheel and rested his head on them. He was tired of being tired. *God, please help me. And please be with Jayden. Keep him safe, and please bring him home.*

# CHAPTER 7

*T*he week passed slowly, and by the time Friday came, Tessa was looking forward to the weekend. But first she and Ben had a meeting with Preston Iken. He had news. As she waited for a bus to take her to Preston's city office for the eleven a.m. meeting, she prayed the news would be positive, but had a sinking feeling it wasn't.

Ben stood outside on the busy pavement when she alighted ten minutes later. He leaned down and kissed her cheek, and she took his hand and squeezed it. They took the lift to the fifth floor in silence.

The receptionist offered coffee. They thanked her politely. The eleven o'clock news beeps sounded from the radio on her desk. Ben crossed his legs at the ankle and then changed them back. He shifted in his seat. Tessa squeezed his hand again. Her own heart was beating faster than normal. If only Preston would hurry up. Soon they'd know one way or the other—had their application been accepted or not?

The receptionist delivered their coffee and directed them into a meeting room. She placed their coffees on the table. "Mr. Iken will be with you shortly." She left. The clock on the wall ticked loudly. After what seemed minutes, but was actually no longer than thirty seconds, Preston bustled into the room, a manila folder tucked under his arm.

"Good morning, Ben, Tessa. Sorry to keep you waiting."

Ben rose and shook Preston's hand.

Preston settled himself in the large leather armchair, placed the folder on the desk, and adjusted his glasses. Leaning forward, he met Ben's gaze over the top of his bi-focals and paused.

"I'm afraid I don't have wonderful news."

Tessa reached out for Ben's hand. It was cold and clammy when she squeezed it.

"The application was rejected because you don't have custody, Ben."

Tessa's shoulders slumped. Exactly what she'd been dreading.

Beside her, Ben remained rigid, as if he were having trouble processing Preston's words. She closed her eyes and swallowed. The small progress Ben had made this week would now be under threat. How would he handle this devastating news? Her heart cried for him. She exhaled slowly and leaned closer to him.

Preston continued. "I know this is disappointing, but we tried our best. The only avenue now is to seek custody, but as Jayden's fifteen, the court will take into consideration his preference." Preston paused. There was no need to state the obvious. Jayden had chosen to live with his mum. Preston cleared his throat. "Go home and think about it, and let me know if you'd like to pursue that option." He removed his glasses and shifted in his seat, his voice softening. "I'm so sorry, Ben. I'd hoped it might have snuck through, but given Jayden's age and the lack of a court order, it didn't stand much chance."

Ben drew in a deep breath and let it out slowly. "Thank you for trying." His voice was brittle. Subdued.

"My pleasure. I just wish I had better news." Preston picked up the folder and pushed his chair back. He paused and looked at Ben and then at Tessa. "I meant to ask if you had any questions."

They both shook their heads.

"Well then, just let me know about the custody issue once you've had a think."

"We will. Thank you, Preston." Tessa stood and shook his hand. Ben followed suit.

Once in the lift, Tessa slipped her arms around Ben's waist and drew him close, resting her head on his chest.

Tears stung her eyes when Ben placed his arms around her shoulders and hugged her. It was going to be a long road, but at least they had each other.


LATER THAT EVENING, Tessa knocked softly on Ben's office door and poked her head in. Ben sat in front of his computer, but didn't seem to be working on anything in particular. The glow from the screen was the only light in the semidarkness of the room. She walked up behind him and placed her hand lightly on his shoulder. "Come for a walk?"

He twisted around and leaned back in his chair. The dark

circles had returned, and his face looked pale and drawn. "Sorry, Tess, I really don't feel like it. You go."

She sighed. "Come on, Ben, it'll do you good." She tried to remain patient and calm. He'd hardly said a word after the morning's meeting with Preston.

He held out his hand. "Maybe tomorrow. Okay?"

Tessa sighed. "Suit yourself." She unwound the dogs' leashes from around her hand and stepped back into the yard. She felt like slamming the door, but refrained and closed it quietly behind her. Bindy and Sparky jumped up from the grass. They could barely hold still while she fastened the leashes onto their green and yellow collars. Despite their eagerness and enthusiasm, she couldn't share in it.

As she left the house and started down the tree-lined path to the dog park, tears she'd been holding back broke free and poured down her face. The ebbing warmth of the evening air had no bearing on her, and even though Bindy and Sparky accompanied her, she felt alone. She gulped as she wiped her tears away. *Will we ever be happy again, God?* She'd been trying to keep positive for Ben's sake, but it was wearing her down. All the hopes and dreams she and Ben had of surrounding themselves with laughing, happy children were now dashed. First the miscarriage, and now Jadyen. Tessa sighed heavily. She'd even started to wonder if God was listening to her prayers. Especially after this morning.

When she reached the park, she unleashed Bindy and Sparky and let them run free. She remained close by them, tossing their balls every now and then, but didn't find their antics as amusing as she normally did. Maybe she needed to talk with someone herself. But who?

*Stephanie.*

She brightened immediately. Caught up in her own troubles, it had been a number of weeks since she'd talked with Stephanie or her mother, but now that Steph was back home on her mother's hobby farm, maybe a visit would be just the thing. She could go first thing in the morning. Ben wouldn't mind.

BEN WAS STILL SLEEPING when Tessa woke the following morning. She'd mentioned her plans to him the night before, and as expected, he encouraged her to go. She dressed quickly and placed a kiss on the top of his head before tiptoeing down the stairs and into her car.

It was a lovely spring morning, the type that made one feel happy to be alive, and beating the heavy traffic that would no doubt clog the highway heading north before too long made it even better. With the city behind her, Tessa began to relax, and by the time she'd reached the lush green Mary Valley a couple of hours later, having spent the time singing along with her favourite CD's, her spirits had lifted and her outlook was more positive.

Pulling into the driveway of 'Misty Morn', Vanessa Trejo's hobby farm, it seemed just yesterday she'd been here to visit Stephanie shortly after the accident. A wide spreading Poinciana tree in full bloom hung over the garden that on Tessa's last visit had been awash with colour. Now, the flowers that had filled the verandah and gardens had been neglected, and instead of brightly coloured petunias, geraniums and daisies, the plants were long and straggly and weighed down by dead heads. Weeds threatened to choke whatever remained of the once beautiful plants. The thought suddenly hit her. That's what was happening with her and Ben. The very life was being choked out of their marriage. Their marriage, which had been so beautiful and wonderful not long ago, was slowly being choked to death by their troubles. The thought made her feel ill in the pit of her stomach. They had to survive this. There was no option—the weeds had to go.

Pausing at the foot of the steps, Tessa steadied herself, inhaling the crisp country air and taking in the beauty of the surroundings. *Lord, please breathe new life into our marriage. And please be with Ben while I'm away.*

She turned, hurried up the steps and knocked on the door.

Mrs. Trejo's eyes lit up when she opened the front door. "What a surprise! It's wonderful to see you, Tessa." She held out her arms and pulled Tessa into an embrace.

Tessa smiled broadly and returned Vanessa's hug. "I hope you don't mind. I probably should have called."

"Don't be silly. Stephanie will be excited to see you. Come in and I'll go wake her."

"Oh, don't do that. I can wait."

"Nonsense. She'll want to see you. Come in and make yourself at home." Mrs. Trejo's voice trailed off as she hurried down the hallway.

Tessa placed her purse on the kitchen table and poured herself a glass of water, gazing out the window at the mountains in the distance. Last time she'd been here, she'd daydreamed about moving to the country, to a place like this. Maybe a change would do her and Ben good, especially if Jayden wasn't coming back.

"Steph will be out in just a bit," Mrs. Trejo said upon returning to the kitchen a few minutes later. Besides a few wrinkles and age spots here and there, she looked the spitting image of her daughter.

"How is she?" Tessa glanced at the doorway, expecting Stephanie to come in at any second.

Mrs. Trejo's expression changed and her eyes misted over. "She can't move her legs at all, and the doctors don't think she'll ever walk again." She lifted her chin. "But apart from that, she's doing well."

Tessa reached out her hand. "Stephanie's a strong girl. She'll come through this."

Mrs. Trejo nodded, dabbing at her nose with a balled up handkerchief she pulled from her apron pocket. "I'm sorry, I still get very emotional when I think about her never being able to lead a normal life again. You know, going out on dates, getting married, having babies." She sniffed. "Walking."

Tessa blinked back tears of her own. "Stephanie's a beautiful person, and even if she never walks again, I'm sure she'll still live a fulfilling life. And you never know who she might meet. I'm sure there's a special person out there who'll love her just the way she is."

Mrs. Trejo responded with a half-smile. Tessa didn't blame her. The likelihood of Stephanie marrying and giving her grandchildren was slim, but it was still early days. And nothing was impossible. Nothing. She herself needed to be reminded of that.

"How's she getting around?" Tessa asked.

As if to answer, Stephanie wheeled herself into the sunroom. Seated in a motorised wheelchair with a brace around one of her legs, Stephanie flashed her old smile. "Hey, Tess."

Tessa's heart leaped. She jumped up and embraced Steph as best she could. "Oh, Steph, it's so good to see you. I should have come earlier."

Stephanie wrinkled her nose as she took a glass of lemonade from her mother. "It's fine, you've been busy." She laughed and caught Tessa's eye before turning away. "It's okay to stare. You're not used to seeing me this way, but I'm okay with it. I haven't let the accident change me, and I'm determined to stay strong even if I never walk again. It could have been a lot worse, you know. I could have died that night, but here I am and here you are. I've never been happier to be alive and I've never appreciated life more."

"You're so brave," Tessa said as she took a seat and squeezed Stephanie's hand. "I'm very proud of you." But was she just putting on a brave face? How could she be so positive and upbeat after what had happened?

"So am I," Mrs. Trejo said. "The doctors may say you'll never walk again, but I have hope that one day you will."

Stephanie shook her head and wagged a finger at her mother. "You and your hoping." She turned to Tessa. "Can you believe it? Mum's done nothing but look up all sorts of treatment options for me since I've been out of the hospital. If I do walk again, I'll have no-one to thank but her."

Tessa looked from the smiling face of Stephanie to her mother's hopeful one. She'd been with them for less than an hour, but the visit was already doing her soul good.

"Come on. Wheel me outside and let's catch up."

Tessa wheeled Stephanie down the ramp, a recent addition,

Steph told her, to a flat grassy area where the views over the valleys to the rolling mountains in the distance took her breath away. She settled Stephanie before she sat on a wooden bench alongside her. As she crossed her legs, she turned to look at her friend.

"So, is it all an act?"

Stephanie burst out in laughter. "You know me so well! But no, it's not an act."

"How are you doing it then? It must be horrible for you."

Stephanie's expression changed. "Yes, it *is* horrible. But you know what? I sincerely meant what I said. It could have been a whole lot worse, but it's given me a deeper appreciation of life, and even when the pain gets really bad, I cope with it. I already feel I'm a stronger person." She shook her head and sighed. "I still can't believe how I acted when I lost my job. I was so immature, and I let it get me down way too much."

Tessa tilted her head. Should she ask? No, it was none of her business. The accident had been assessed as just that. An accident. If Stephanie had really intended to take her life, she'd tell her if she wanted to.

"I'm so impressed with how you're handling it. Better than Ben and I are handling the situation with Jayden." Her voice caught in her throat. She swallowed. How bad would it be to break down in front of Stephanie when it was Stephanie confined to a wheelchair and not her? *Pull yourself together, Tess.*

"Oh Tess. He'll come back, I'm sure of it." Stephanie held her hand out. "Has Ben got his depression back?"

Tessa held a tissue to her eye and nodded.

"Don't you worry. He'll be okay. He's a deep-thinking man,

and it just takes time for him to work through things. Is he seeing another counsellor?"

Tessa nodded again. "Yes, a male this time. Seems okay. But nowhere as good as you." She forced herself to laugh.

"Yeah, right." Stephanie chuckled. "I couldn't even take my own counsel."

"But look at you now. God's going to use you, I'm sure of it."

Stephanie's smile broadened. "Thank you." She paused, and held Tessa's gaze. "Can I share something with you?"

Tessa's heart began to pound. *Surely not...*

Stephanie must have seen the look of alarm on Tessa's face. "No, it's nothing bad. It's good. Pastor Stanek came to visit me in hospital."

Tessa relaxed as visions of the kindly old pastor came to mind.

"He challenged me. He asked if my anchor would hold in the storms of life. He knew it was one of my favourite hymns, and he quoted it back at me. It made me really think about whether my faith was just a fair weather faith, or whether it really would stand up now I was facing a storm. A hurricane, really." Steph let out a small chuckle. "I have to admit it threw me at first, but then I decided. Yes, my anchor would hold. I know it's not going to be easy, but whose life is? We all have our own journeys, some might be a little easier than others, but no-one gets through life on this side of heaven unscathed. So I just recommitted my life to God, and I know he'll give me the strength to live each day, and to be thankful for everything I have." Stephanie drew a slow breath. "Maybe that will help you too."

Tessa couldn't help herself. She burst into tears as memories of Stephanie sitting at the piano at her old church flashed through her mind. She could even remember Stephanie playing that very hymn. How easy it was to sing songs and hymns when everything was fine with your life. But how much more meaningful when things weren't. She blew her nose and turned her gaze to the mountains. How her life had changed since the break-up with Michael. Before then, her biggest challenge had been deciding what career to follow, and in the end, that had been an easy choice. When she'd accepted Ben's proposal, she knew they'd face challenges, but she'd never expected Jayden to disappear with his mum and for their marriage to be under so much pressure so early on. And her miscarriage...

Her heart grew heavy. But Steph was right—what good was a fair-weather faith? God had never promised an easy life. In fact, Jesus himself had said that in this world there would be trouble, but to take heart, because He had overcome the world, and that in Him, peace could be found. Tears pricked her eyes. Would her anchor hold, or would she and Ben be swept away in the storm they were facing? She swallowed hard and squeezed her eyes as Stephanie took her hand.

"It's okay, Tess. God's with you, and He'll carry you and hold you firm. Just like He's doing with me."

Tessa nodded, unable to speak. She determined that her anchor would hold, and prayed that Ben's would too.


BEFORE TESSA LEFT the following day, Stephanie and Tessa sat at the piano while Stephanie played all the old hymns they used to love singing at Gracepointe Church. When Stephanie began to play *Will Your Anchor Hold*, tears rolled down Tessa's cheek as she sang, but without a shadow of a doubt, she knew that her anchor was grounded firm and deep in the Saviour's love, and that despite whatever lay ahead, God was with her and she would make it through. She also weeded the garden with Stephanie's mum.

# CHAPTER 8

*W*hen Ben woke on Saturday morning and Tessa wasn't there, he toyed with the idea of rolling over and going back to sleep. In fact, he was tempted to stay there all day. The lump that had formed in his stomach after hearing Preston's news still lay heavy, and he just wanted to curl up and hide from the world. Jayden would never be coming home now. Regardless of Tessa's constant optimism, the reality was that he'd messed up, and he'd lost his son. Forever. The pain in his chest was suffocating. The counsellor's words flashed through his mind, *'Try not to dwell on what's happened. You can't change that. The only things you can change are your attitudes, thoughts and reactions to what's happened.'*

Ben sighed and threw off the bedcovers. He placed his feet on the floor and perched on the edge of the bed. He placed his head in his hands. *God, I'm giving You the situation. Please help me change my thinking, and help me get through this. You know how heavy my heart is and how bad I feel. I don't know how to move forward, but I'll trust You. A day at a time. Thank you.*

He stepped into the shower, and as the warm water flowed over his body, some of his pain slipped away. When he stepped out, the cloud that had been his constant companion since the day Jayden left had lifted a little.

He'd been neglecting his daily Bible reading, but today he opened his Bible as he ate breakfast—outside on the deck with Bindy and Sparky lying next to him. Filtered sunshine reached him through the surrounding bushes and trees which seemed to have shot up all of a sudden. He blinked. Last time he'd noticed, they weren't that big. How long had it been since he'd trimmed them? He quickly finished breakfast and found the electric trimmer in the garage and began trimming. By the time he finished, the pile of garden waste was almost as tall as himself. Just as well they had a large garden bag. He bundled it up and carried it in several lots to the bag, all the while trying not to trip over the dogs. With Tessa gone, he probably had little choice but to take them out. After a quick break, he found their leashes and headed down the street towards the park.

He sidestepped around a young boy who'd stopped in the middle of the path on his training bike.

The boy's father raced towards him and pushed the bike out of Ben's way. "Sorry." He gave Ben an apologetic look.

"No problem." Ben smiled at him as Bindy and Sparky stopped for a pat from the boy. "How old's your son?"

"Three. He keeps us on our toes." The man chuckled.

Ben gave the man a wistful smile as a memory of pushing Jayden on a training bike not too dissimilar from this one flashed through his mind. "Enjoy him. He'll grow up too quick-ly." Pulling the dogs away from the boy, Ben gave a nod and continued his walk.

He let Bindy and Sparky take the lead and followed without thinking about where they were taking him. How had time passed so quickly? It didn't seem that long ago since Jayden was just a little boy, learning to ride a bike. He pushed the memory away. No use dwelling on the past, especially when it would only make him sad again.

As he neared the river, the ringing of his phone sounded from his pocket. He stopped and pulled it out. A message from Eleanor. He clicked on it. *Hi Ben. We know Tess is away, so wondering if you'd like to join us for dinner at Bussey's tonight?* Ben's shoulders slumped. Tessa's parents meant well, but could he handle being with them on his own without her there? Was he ready to begin talking with people again? He drew a slow breath, his gaze fixed on a ferry chugging slowly across the river. He should go. If he was determined to make changes, this would be the perfect opportunity to start. He hit reply and accepted.

LATER THAT AFTERNOON, Ben made his way to Bussey's Seafood Restaurant. Eleanor and Telford were already seated, and waved to him when he arrived. He gave Eleanor a kiss and shook Telford's hand before taking his seat.

"Guess you heard about the application?"

Eleanor touched his wrist lightly. "Yes, and we're so sorry."

Ben swallowed hard, pushing down the lump in his throat. "We kind of expected it, but getting a final answer was hard."

"We can't imagine how you're feeling," Telford said, his big bushy eyebrows moving in time with his mouth. "It's hard enough for us with Elliott away, but he's a grown man."

Ben lowered his gaze to his hands.

"Telford, we agreed not to talk about it." Eleanor's voice was little more than a whisper.

Ben looked up. "It's okay. I've got to learn to deal with it, and to talk about it."

"We're all praying for you, son," Telford said.

"Thank you." Ben gave them both an appreciative smile.

"Shall we order?" Telford pulled the menus from the holder in the middle of the table and passed them out. "Not that we really need to look."

Eleanor chuckled at her husband as a familiar, comfortable look passed between them, tugging at Ben's heart. Would he and Tess look at each other like that after thirty years of marriage? He hoped so.

They ordered, and then chatted about things in general, until the conversation turned back to Jayden.

"We pray for him everyday, Ben. That he'll make good decisions, and that harm won't come his way. He's a good boy, and he knows deep down where his family is." Eleanor tapped Ben on the wrist again. "He'll come home one day. I'm sure of it."

"That's what Tessa keeps saying. But I'm not so sure."

"I've got some verses for you. You've been on my heart for weeks now, and I feel strongly that God wants me to share these verses with you. May I?" Eleanor's warm, caring expression tugged at his heart. He'd grown to admire this woman, and any word of comfort or wisdom she could impart was more than welcome.

"Sure."

She smiled broadly at him. "They're from 2nd Corinthians 4, verses 16 to 18. You probably already know them, *'Therefore we do not lose heart. Though outwardly we are wasting away, yet inwardly we are being renewed day by day. For our light and momentary troubles are achieving for us an eternal glory that far outweighs them all. So we fix our eyes not on what is seen, but on what is unseen, since what is seen is temporary, but what is unseen is eternal.'* She touched his arm again lightly and held his gaze. "We don't know what's going to happen with Jayden, but God does. And we have to trust Him. In the meantime, I pray that you and Tessa will grow stronger together, and that God will renew you both inwardly every day. Fix your eyes on God, and allow Him to do a wonderful work in your life. Telford and I would hate to see this situation tear you apart. Draw strength from God, and be assured He'll never let you face more than you can bear." She leaned back. "There, I've said more than I intended, I'm sorry."

"It's okay. Thank you. That means so much, and I'll certainly take it on board." Ben squeezed her hand and gave her a warm smile.

On his way home, he let those verses play over again in his mind. He didn't really think his troubles were that light or momentary, but in the whole scheme of things, he guessed they were. He was on a journey, and this trouble was part of that journey. Two choices confronted him; be swallowed by his troubles, or fix his eyes firmly on Jesus, allowing Him to work in his heart along this journey that had been thrust upon him. Ben's spirit moved within him as the answer became clear. There was no choice. As challenging as it might be, he would fix his eyes on Jesus and not allow his troubles to engulf him any longer.

# CHAPTER 9

*O*n Sunday afternoon, Tessa headed back home in much better spirits. A thought was slowly beginning to grow inside her. A thought that made her heart pound with excitement, and she was almost convinced it was from God. Of course, she'd pray about it some more, and then she'd have to tell Ben. That would be the difficult part. Ben wasn't a very go-with-the-flow type of person and wasn't that keen on unexpected changes. He preferred to plan and stick to schedules. She sometimes wished he were more spontaneous and flexible, but maybe if he were, she'd then wish he wasn't. Well, she would just have to take a chance and hope he'd agree with her idea.

When she pulled into the driveway, she was surprised to see Margaret walking away from the front door. "Margaret, I'm glad you're here." Tessa jumped out of the car and hugged her. "I've got something to run past you."

"Only after you let me inside so I can sit down and give my

feet a rest. I've been ringing the doorbell and knocking for a good ten minutes now. I even tried calling you." Margaret took off her wide-brimmed sun hat and fanned her face.

"Oh, I'm sorry." Tessa hurried to unlock the door and led the way into the living room. "I've been visiting Stephanie and her mother, and my phone died. I forgot to take my charger. Ben should be home anyway." She called out, but he didn't answer. She didn't even receive a response from Bindy or Sparky. "I guess not. He probably took the dogs for a walk. Take a seat and I'll get you some water."

Margaret settled onto a couch while Tessa disappeared into the kitchen.

It didn't take her long to fill two glasses with iced water and return to the living room. In her hand, Margaret held a framed photo of Ben and Jayden taken at the wedding. Tessa smiled sadly and sat down on the couch beside her. "Do you think Jayden will come back?"

Margaret patted Tessa's leg. "Of course he will. He's probably not ready to admit it yet, but deep in his heart, Jayden knows that you and Ben love him. He knows this is home." She set the photo back down and took her glass of water, taking hold of Tessa's hand with her free one. "That's why I came over. I wanted to see how you've been holding up. Have you heard anything from him yet?"

"Not directly. He contacts Neil, but he won't reply to any of our emails or texts. Ben's called him like a thousand times." Tessa sighed. "It's like he wants to forget we even exist."

"Don't talk like that. Give him time."

"Yes, I know. I'm sorry." How quickly she'd lost the confidence and peace she'd felt after being with Stephanie and her mum. Why couldn't she be as steady and hopeful about the future as they were?

"And how have you and Ben been holding up?" Margaret's expression grew more serious.

Tessa remained quiet for a few moments before answering. She exhaled heavily. "Not very well, I'm afraid. That's why I went to see Stephanie. I had to get away from all this." She waved her hand around the sunlit living room. "Everything here reminds us of Jayden, and Ben and I-" She stopped. A flush crept across her cheeks. "Well, Ben and I are barely talking to one another. When we're both home, we're like ships in the night. We hardly spend any quality time together. Ever since Jayden left, Ben's been spending more time at the office, even on weekends when he doesn't have to work. And after Friday, when we got the news about the application..." She teared up.

Margaret's eyes softened and she took hold of Tessa's hand. "We're all praying for you, dear."

Tessa swallowed hard and gave Margaret the best smile she could manage.

"Thank you, I appreciate it." She drew in a slow breath to steady herself. "Let me make some tea." She disappeared into the kitchen and switched the kettle on. She needed a moment to settle her thoughts. Her mind was racing ahead of itself, but for the first time since Jayden had left, she felt she had some direction, but she needed to run her idea past Margaret in case it was totally unrealistic.

Tessa was pouring the tea when Margaret joined her in the kitchen.

"Shall we sit outside?"

"Yes, why not?" Tessa handed Margaret a mug of steaming tea and picked up her own, along with a plate of shop-bought Anzac biscuits, and followed Margaret outside. Tessa's eyes popped. The bushes had all been trimmed. *They weren't like that when I left.* A smile formed on her face at the thought of Ben actually doing this.

"This is lovely, dear," Margaret said as she gazed around the yard.

"Yes, it is, thank you. We loved it when we first moved in, but now..."

Margaret patted her hand and looked at her with a kindly expression. "I know a little of how you're feeling. All those years when Harrison wouldn't have anything to do with Harold and me. Nothing hurts more than having a child who acts like you don't exist."

Tessa nodded and wrapped her hands around the warm mug. "I think I'm okay now, after the weekend with Stephanie. But I'm concerned about Ben. He's started counselling, but so far it doesn't seem to have made much difference. And the decision we got on Friday really threw him."

"I'm not a counsellor, but maybe you and Ben need to get away for a while." Margaret's voice was soft and caring. "Nothing fancy, but I'm sure a break would do you good. Somewhere different where you're not reminded of Jayden all the time. Not that you want to forget him, but being away from here would help you to regain your focus on God and on each other."

Tessa's pulse quickened. She looked up and took a quick breath. "That's exactly what I've been thinking since being with Stephanie. I feel God's placed this idea on my heart. Please tell me if this is crazy or not... I had this thought that we should go on a mission trip to get a new perspective on everything. If we just went on a holiday, we'd still be thinking about Jayden all the time, and I don't see it would help, but if we went on a mission trip, I think it'd help get our minds off ourselves and Jayden, at least for a while. I haven't thought where we'd go or for how long, but I just feel it's something we should do. Of course, Ben would have to agree."

Margaret squeezed Tessa's hand and smiled broadly. "I think the mission trip's a wonderful idea, and Ben just might think the same. You won't know until you ask him."

# CHAPTER 10

Soon after Margaret left, the eager yaps of Bindy and Sparky announced Ben's return. Tessa scooped up the stack of papers she'd printed out and stepped into the backyard. Since sharing with Margaret, she'd been praying for God to give Ben a positive heart towards the mission trip idea. Now the time had come for her to tell him about it. She hoped Margaret was right and that he'd be as excited about the idea as she was.

Taking Sparky's leash, Tessa leaned up and gave him a kiss. "Good to see you up and about, sweetie."

"These two didn't give me much option. Persistent creatures." Ben let out a small chuckle as he unclipped Bindy's leash. "They were about to have a fit if someone didn't take them to the park. Almost wore me out."

"And was it you who trimmed the bushes?" She sidled up to him, slipping her arms around his waist and leaning back as she met his gaze.

Ben's eyes twinkled. "So you noticed?" He raised an eyebrow.

"How could I not? There's not much left of them!"

He laughed as he leaned down and kissed her slowly on the lips.

Her heart skipped a beat. Where had this come from? Such a welcome and unexpected change, but giving hope that he'd be open to her idea. She reluctantly pulled away and filled the dogs' bowls with water, all the while trying to keep her excitement under control.

"How's Stephanie?" Ben poured out an equal amount of food for both dogs but glanced at her as he did. Bindy and Sparky yapped as they ran back and forth waiting for their dinner.

Tessa smiled as she watched them, then lifted her gaze. "Much better than I'd expected. She can't use her legs, but she and her mum are so optimistic about the future. It's strange, but the accident has helped Stephanie to see things differently. She's got a much better outlook now than after she lost her job."

"That's great." Ben picked up the dogs' bowls and held them above the jumping dogs before placing them on the ground. "I can't imagine what it would be like."

"I know, but she's doing well. She really is." She took a deep breath. *Here goes.* "When I was driving back from the farm, I had an idea." She held her breath as she held up a picture of an Ecuadorian village she'd printed out.

Ben stepped closer, drawing his brows together. "Ecuador? What's this about?"

Tessa gulped. "With all that's happened with Jayden leaving,

I think it'd be good for us to take some time away, to regain our focus on God and on each other. I hate how we've been." She stepped closer, and lifted her hands to Ben's chest as she gazed into his surprised eyes. "I feel God's put this idea into my head, so let me speak. I think it'd help us get a new perspective on everything, and I've always wanted to go on a mission trip. After praying about it, Ecuador popped into my mind. It wouldn't have to be for long, maybe one or two months at the most, but I'm sure we could stay longer if we wanted."

Ben remained silent.

Tessa held her breath. What would he say?

"I don't know. You've taken me by surprise. Ecuador's a long way from Australia, and what if Jayden comes back while we're there? His ninety days will be up soon."

"We'd come back if he did; it's only a flight away. We need to get away from here, and it shouldn't be difficult to organise. Elliott's already there, and I'm sure he'd help us apply and get everything sorted. Think about it?" She tilted her head. What was he thinking? If he agreed, it would be a huge step, but one she believed would be so beneficial.

Ben sat down and flipped through the papers, stopping every now and then to read some of the information. "I guess it might be good." He raised his head.

Tessa's pulse raced.

"I agree we should get away, but Ecuador? What if Jayden does decide to come home? It's so far away."

She sat and took his hand, holding his gaze. "I fully believe Jayden will come back, hopefully sooner than later, but to be honest, I don't think it'll be for some time yet, even with his ninety days almost up." She paused and took a breath. She was talking too fast. "Jayden knows where we are, and if he wanted to come back by now, he would have done so. He wouldn't be ignoring us the way he has if he was wanting to come back soon. And if he does come back while we're away, we'll just jump on a plane. I'm sure Elliott and the others would understand. And maybe we could try to visit him on our way back... it's not far from Florida." She was being a little cheeky throwing that in, but if it helped?

Ben set the papers aside and rested his chin in his hand. After a few minutes of silence, he lifted his head and met Tessa's gaze.

Her heart beat louder and faster. She sensed God was at work in both their hearts. Just the fact that Ben's outlook had improved so much over the weekend was encouragement enough, but now...

"Okay, as long as we can maintain email contact just in case Jayden does decide to come back, I think going on a mission trip together will do us good."

"Oh, Ben!" Tessa threw her arms around him so suddenly he nearly toppled over. She could hardly put her happiness into words.


THE NEXT MONTH or so was a flurry of activity as Ben and Tessa prepared to leave their house in New Farm and fly to Ecuador. Christmas came and went. At least planning the trip helped to take their minds off the empty chair around the table when they had Christmas lunch with her parents. They tried to call Jayden late on Christmas night, but his phone didn't even ring—the number was no longer active. And there was no reply to the email Ben sent. The Facebook message also remained unseen.

Ben wrapped up the projects he'd been working on and left his clients in Walton's capable hands. Tessa put Harrison back in charge at the clinic and left Bindy and Sparky with her parents who happily agreed to look after the dogs while they were away. They decided to sublet their house to a couple who'd recently moved from Canberra to be closer to their daughter, assuring Ben and Tessa that the house and yard would be kept in good condition. After applying and being accepted through Mission to the World, Elliott's mission agency, and after getting some tips from Elliott on what to expect and what they should bring, Ben and Tessa were soon packed and on a plane ready to embark on the greatest adventure of their lives.

# CHAPTER 11

*A* month had passed, and Jayden still felt like a fish out of water at Miranda High. Keith had snubbed him—the school's unspoken rule was clear; sophomores and seniors didn't mix. The only sports teams they had were basketball, football, and baseball—none of which he played. Some of the students, and even some of the teachers, still asked about his accent which they thought was either funny or cute. He didn't understand why the way he talked was such a big deal.

But at least he'd made one good friend, although hanging out with Raymond Astey wouldn't help him make any more. Quiet and bespectacled, Raymond was the nerd of the class. He wasn't into sport, but loved Science and Math. Dad would be happy about that.

"Can you show me your jet ski today?" Raymond asked him one day after school as they took their books out of their lockers.

"Sure. Mum's not picking me up, so we'll have to walk."

Raymond shrugged. "That's fine. My parents never pick me up. I usually walk home anyway."

The two boys slung their bags over their shoulders and began the twenty-minute walk, chatting the entire time about the physics assignment that was due in three days' time.

Jayden's eyes widened as he and Raymond rounded the corner and entered his street. A large moving truck was parked beside Mum's car. A lump grew in his stomach. What was going on? *Maybe it's for the people next door.* But they had their own driveways. The truck was in theirs.

"What's wrong?" Raymond looked at him, forehead puckered.

"Not sure."

They approached the truck. The back was open. Jayden peered inside as they squeezed past. A row of stacked boxes filled the back, and on the side, several large pictures that had been hanging on Mum's bedroom wall were covered in plastic and strapped to some framework. Jayden blinked. What was happening? Surely they weren't moving? He ran to the elevator and punched the button for the second floor.

Raymond followed. "Should I leave?"

"No. Come up. I just need to find out what's going on." Jayden tried to keep his voice lighthearted, but knew he wasn't succeeding.

He took his key out but didn't need it. The door was already open and Mum stood just inside it, talking to one of the movers. "What's going on, Mum?" He tried to keep his voice calm, but his heart pounded.

"Oh, hi Jay. How was school?" She placed an arm around his

shoulder. He shrugged it off. How could she sound as if nothing unusual was happening?

"Fine." His brows hooded

"I see you've brought a friend." She gave Raymond one of her over-the-top smiles.

"Yeah, this is Raymond. I wouldn't have brought him if I'd known all our stuff was being packed up."

"I meant to tell you yesterday, Jay, but there were still a few loose ends that had to be tied up. I've sold the condo and the boat, and we're moving to Texas."

"Texas? Why?" Jayden strode past her and stared at the empty walls and rearranged furniture that was being broken down and packed away.

"I found a job with a golf fashion magazine. It starts in a week, so we have to move tomorrow. Sorry for the short notice, Jay, but I had to make a quick decision. I hope you understand."

No, he didn't understand. Why should he? She'd told him she was rich. Didn't need to work. So why all of a sudden did she need a job? And what about the private plane? Wasn't that hers?

"Whatever," he said quietly, more to himself than to her. He rubbed the back of his neck and sighed. "Guess I've got to go?"

"Of course. I wouldn't leave you here on your own."

"I was going to take Raymond for a ride on the jet ski. Have you sold that too?"

Her expression gave him the answer. She grabbed his hand. "I'm sorry, Jay. It had to go."

He shook his head. "I don't believe it. Bet you've sold my guitar, too."

"I'll leave." Raymond backed out of the door and disappeared down the hallway. Jayden didn't blame him. How many mothers would do this to their children?

It took Kathryn and Jayden two days to drive from Florida to Austin, Texas, stopping only for gas, food, and an overnight stay in a hotel. Jayden slunk in his seat most of the way, listening to his music.

Arriving on the outskirts of the city in the early afternoon, Kathryn nudged Jayden awake. "Come on Jay, be interested. We're almost there."

He pulled himself up and removed his earphones. They were still on the freeway, but in the distance, high-rise buildings poked their heads out through a haze of smog, as if they were floating in thin air. Cars whizzed by on either side as Mum slowed a little.

"Know where we're going?" Jayden turned his head.

Sitting forward in her seat, his mother had a tight grip on the steering wheel, the veins in her neck as taut as the strings on his guitar which for some strange reason she hadn't sold. She still wore her large sunglasses, but her whole demeanor was strained.

"Following the navigator. Should be there in ten minutes."

'There' turned out to be a nondescript apartment building in the middle of suburbia. Nowhere near the water, and nothing like the condo they'd just left.

"How did you find this place?" Jayden's nose wrinkled as he opened the door to the second-floor apartment not much bigger than the bedroom he'd just left.

"On the Internet." She pushed past him and drew in a slow breath as her gaze travelled around the room. "It'll do." Her mouth was set in a hard line.

"Why did we have to move, Mum?"

Her lower lip quivered, her eyes misting over. "Let's just say that Luke didn't keep his word."

As much as Jayden didn't want to be here, he felt sorry for her and softened his tone. "Guess it'll be okay."

She held out her hand to him and smiled through her tears. "Thank you, Jay."

Jayden shrugged. *Whatever.* He sighed as he carried his bag to the smaller of the two bedrooms and opened the window to let some fresh air in. Instead of the sound of boats and jet skis and children splashing in water, the drone of traffic reached his ears. Somewhere in the distance a siren wailed. Mum had told him that Austin was a great place to live, but if he was honest, he just wanted to go home to Dad and Tessa. Tears rolled down his cheeks as he began unpacking. It was all such a mess. And what was worse—he had to start another new school.

# CHAPTER 12

On Jayden's first day at Hillview High, a boy called Roger befriended him. Roger lived in the same apartment building and was in the same class for most subjects. They caught the bus to school together each morning and back each afternoon. Jayden probably wouldn't have chosen Roger as his best friend if he'd had a choice. He was a bit too cool for Jayden's liking, but still, it was better to have a friend like Roger than none at all.

Kathryn began her job but often worked late, some nights not arriving home until after Jayden was in bed. Sometimes she woke him when she stumbled in well after midnight. After several weeks, Jayden had had enough and sat up and waited for her. He fell asleep on the couch, but was awakened by the key turning in the door. He opened his eyes and watched her come in.

She swayed on her feet as she made her way towards the couch. She dropped her purse on the coffee table and kicked off her shoes, and was about to flop onto the couch on top of him.

Jayden moved out of the way quickly. She jumped back, startled, nearly losing her footing.

"What are you doing up?" Her voice was slurred.

"Waiting for you to come home." Jayden's eyes narrowed as he took in her bloodshot eyes and disheveled appearance.

"You should be in bed." She wobbled on her feet.

"And you should have been home hours ago." Jayden's chest heaved. *So this is what she does every night.*

"I was working."

"*Until one in the morning?*"

"I was with clients. Let me sit."

He shifted and made space for her. She flopped onto the couch and leaned her head on his shoulder.

"Be a good boy and get me a drink." She hiccupped.

Jayden lifted her head off his shoulder. "No way. You've had enough to drink already."

"Don't be a spoil-sport." She reached up, draping her hand over his head.

"I'm going to bed, and so should you." He tried to stand. She pulled him back. He glared at her. "When are you going to stop doing this to yourself, Mum? You were late for work yesterday because you were out drinking the night before. If you keep this up, you're going to be out of a job, and then what are we going to do?"

She sighed wearily and patted his hand. "Stop worrying, Jay. I'm not going to lose my job." She hiccupped again.

"You will if you keep drinking." Jayden crossed his arms, his glare holding firm.

"Go to bed, Jay." She rubbed her forehead. "I have a headache. I need to sleep it off." She pulled herself up and held on to the furniture to steady herself as she moved past him and stumbled down the darkened hallway and into her bedroom.

Jayden blinked back tears. What would happen if Mum did lose her job and their money ran out? Already things were tight and often the pantry and fridge were next to empty. Back home, he'd never even paid a thought to shopping for groceries or paying bills or having a place to stay. He'd never been concerned about Dad or Tessa losing their jobs. He'd just taken it all for granted. If he could bring himself to admit to Dad and Tessa that he'd made a mistake, maybe he could go home. But how could he leave Mum on her own now? Jayden sighed heavily as he plodded down the hallway to his bed.

SEVERAL HOURS LATER, Jayden woke to his alarm buzzing in his ear. It didn't seem as if he'd slept at all, but he must have had at least a few hours. He dragged himself out of bed and knocked on Mum's door. She didn't stir. Why should he have to wake her anyway? She was his mother, and she should be the one waking him, not the other way around. He drew a breath and walked the few steps to the bathroom.

Once showered and dressed, he opened the fridge. An open bottle of wine, some butter, a milk bottle with only a tiny bit of milk left, and a few bits of stale bread were the only contents. He closed it. He already knew what was in the pantry, so didn't even bother looking. He'd go without, again.

Roger was standing at the bus stop eating a box of breakfast tarts when Jayden arrived a few minutes later, his bag slung over his shoulder.

"Hey Jayden. Want some?" Roger held the box out.

"I won't say no. Thanks."

"No problem. Hey, d'you want to come over for dinner again tonight? We're having spaghetti and meatballs." Roger stuffed the last piece of his breakfast tart into his mouth, and then squashed the box under his foot.

"As long as that's cool with your mum." Jayden pulled open a tart and held it in front of his mouth. "Cause my mum won't mind." *She probably won't even be home.*

"You mean my *mom?*" Sometimes Roger teased him about his accent, but jokingly. He was never mean. "Yeah, she's cool." Roger cocked his head. "So what did you think? You don't look any different. Do you feel different?"

Jayden popped the tart into his mouth and then opened his bag, pulling out a Ziploc sandwich bag containing several pills from an inner compartment. "I didn't take any."

"Why not?" Roger drew his eyebrows together.

Jayden shrugged. "Just don't see the need, that's all. I told you that."

"Suit yourself, but you know what the other guys are going to say. You won't even have a drink. You need to loosen up, man."

Jayden's shoulders slumped. How much longer could he stay strong? Taking drugs and getting drunk was wrong, he knew that. He couldn't forget the time he'd overdosed and was rushed to hospital. No way did he want that to happen again. His Sunday School teacher at Fellowship Bible Church had talked a lot about the difference between right and wrong, and how important it was for young people to stand up for what was right, even when their peers pressured them to do the opposite. Even though he hadn't been to church of late, every time Jayden felt pressured to join in with his new friends, a voice in his head told him not to. But he certainly wasn't about to tell Roger that.

Jayden handed the pills back to Roger. "Whenever my mum drinks, she acts weird. I don't want to turn out like that."

"That's probably because your mom drinks too much. You don't have to get drunk. You can just drink a little. C'mon, just a taste isn't going to hurt you."

Jayden shrugged, breathing a sigh of relief as the long, yellow bus turned into the street. Why did he have to have conversations like this with Roger? And why couldn't he just fit in without being pressured? It wasn't right.

Roger climbed into the bus behind Jayden. "There's a pool party at Britney's house tomorrow. You should come."

Jayden's face sagged. Just as well Roger couldn't see it. He probably couldn't get out of going, having made excuses for every party he'd been invited to since arriving. If he didn't go, he'd really be on the outs with Roger. And he didn't want that. Taking his seat, Jayden lifted his gaze and forced a smile. "Okay. It sounds great. I'll be there."

# CHAPTER 13

*T*he pool party was in full swing when Jayden
arrived at Britney's expansive, two-story house the
following evening. Music blasted from a portable stereo
system, and about a hundred young people, spread between
the patio and the yard, danced or stood in groups chatting.

"Glad you made it." Roger clapped him on the back and
handed him a red plastic cup.

Jayden sniffed the semi-clear liquid, jerking his head back
as the whiff of alcohol reached his nose. Roger and some other
boys from his class stood watching. He didn't want to do this,
but took a sip just to keep face. The liquid had a tang, stinging
his taste buds and burning his throat as it slid down. He spat
most of it back into the cup.

Roger laughed and clapped him on the back. "You'll get
used to it. Take it slowly."

Jayden took another sip. This time it went down easier.

A girl wearing very short hot pants ran by and linked arms with Roger, dragging him away.

Roger looked back over his shoulder, spilling the drink he was carrying in his free hand. "Sorry. I'll be back soon."

Left to himself, Jayden wandered across to the pool area. A game of volleyball was in full swing.

"The girls are totally winning this." A blonde in a hot pink swimsuit stood beside him.

Jayden couldn't help but admire her curves. And her long legs. And her sparkling blue eyes. He swallowed hard. "You must be Britney."

Her eyes twinkled as she flashed him a brilliant smile. "I am. And you must be Jayden. Roger told me about you. You have that neat accent thing going on. Are you going to finish that?" She pointed to the cup in his hand.

"I don't think so."

She took the cup and sculled the remainder.

Jayden's eyes widened. *How did she do that?*

"What?" She gave him a quizzical look and then laughed.

"Nothing." Jayden struggled for something to say. He glanced around. "You... you have a nice place." *That sounds so pathetic.*

"Why, thank you! My parents are gone for the week, so I pretty much have it to myself." Her smile morphed into a coy grin. "What are you looking at me like that for? Do you think I'm attractive?" Her voice was soft and gooey like honey. She placed her hand on her hip and leaned her chest towards him.

Jayden gulped. He was way out of his league. "I... I guess so."

"Wanna see inside the house?" She grabbed his arm. "Some of the girls are having some serious fun in there."

His pulse raced. *I can imagine what kind of fun they're having.* He tried to ply her hand off his arm, but she was stronger than she looked and dragged him along.

"Can't we stay out here? Play some volleyball?"

"Don't be a spoil-sport, Jayden."

Once inside, it took a few moments for his eyes to adjust. The inside of the house seemed spacious—more spacious than any house he'd ever lived in, and way bigger than the dingy apartment he was now living in with Mum. The room was hazy, with the familiar odor of pot lingering in the air. Ghostly figures moved about. And to his right, a couple were making out on a couch. *Enough.* He had to get out of here.

Britney leaned in closer and plucked at his shirt. "Let's go to my bedroom. It's less crowded there."

Sweat broke out on his forehead. He jerked his arm away. "No. I have to go." His head spun as he retraced his steps to the back door.

"What's wrong?" Britney followed after him, grabbing his arm.

He shrugged her off. "Must have been something I ate. I don't feel too well." It wasn't true, but it was the best excuse he could come up with quickly.

Not waiting to say goodbye to Roger, he snuck out through a side gate and slowly made his way back on foot to his apartment. His eyes blurred with tears as the music faded into the distance. Why couldn't he just fit in? He so desperately wanted to be accepted, but not if it meant doing what was wrong.

It took half an hour, and he hardly noticed the other people wandering the streets. Reaching the apartment, he stopped on the front stoop and looked up at the sky. A full moon shone brightly, making it almost like daytime. He sat on the step and hung his head between his hands.

If only he had someone to talk to, someone who could help him sort through his mixed up emotions and give him advice. But there was no-one. Talking to Mum would be a waste of time. She didn't have it together. He'd left it too long to talk with Dad. Neil was about the only one, but it seemed Neil had made new friends and wasn't talking much these days. *What about God?* The quiet voice inside Jayden's head made his heart race. Dad had once told him it didn't matter where he was or how he felt, if he prayed hard enough, God would always hear him and answer him. Maybe he should give it a try.

Jayden lifted his gaze to the sky. "Dear God ... " his shoulders slumped. The words just wouldn't come. Besides, why would God listen to him? He'd never really prayed before. He didn't even like going to church. He didn't have a personal connection with God like Ben and Tessa had. He'd run away from home, and now he was being tempted to drink and do drugs. *No, God doesn't want to hear from me, much less answer me.* Dropping his head again, he closed his eyes and let out a defeated sigh. When he began to shiver, he dragged himself up and made his way to bed. He didn't even notice if Mum was home.

WHEN HE AWOKE the next morning, she was in the laundry room folding towels. Jayden raised his eyebrows. *She mustn't have gone out drinking last night. Amazing.* He yawned as he stood just outside the door.

"Good morning, Jay. About time you got out of bed." She paused, tilting her head. "What's up?"

He looked up in surprise. How did she know he had something on his mind? Maybe he could try talking to her after all. Couldn't hurt. He entered the laundry room and turned over an empty clothesbasket and sat on it. "Nothing much really." He nibbled his fingernails and glanced at her. "I was just wondering..." He cocked his head. "What do you believe in, Mum?"

Her eyes shot open. "What do you mean?"

"Like, do you believe in God, or prayer? And what do you think life's all about?"

She shrugged, her face blank. She stared down at the purple towel in her hands. "I used to go to church years ago, but I never got much out of it. As for God," she shrugged, "I just don't know." She started folding the towel. "I mean, I sure do hope that some greater being is out there watching over the world and making sure nothing gets too messed up, but I think we're pretty much on our own. We live. We learn. It's really up to us to figure out life, and I certainly haven't figured it all out yet, so -" Her voice trailed off as she shrugged again and picked up another towel.

*That was a lot of help.* Jayden's gaze clouded over as he rubbed his forehead and walked into the kitchen. Once again, his thoughts turned to Dad and Tessa. They knew who they believed in and they knew who they were. They went to church, and always seemed to get something worthwhile out of it. Their lives held meaning, even when things didn't quite turn out the way they wanted. Even though Dad had been strict, *too strict,* and sometimes Tessa had been too soft, they loved him. *And they still love me.* A heavy weight grew in his stomach. It had been a big mistake leaving them to be with Mum. It might not be true, but she really did seem to be using him to fill a hole in her life.

# CHAPTER 14

"ey Jayden, did you hear?" Roger ambled down the hallway chewing gum. Jayden closed the door of the apartment and fell into step.

"Hear what?" Jayden stifled a yawn. Last night he'd emptied all of Kathryn's bottles down the sink in a desperate effort to stop her drinking, but it had backfired. She'd caught him red-handed and yelled at him and they'd argued long into the night. She stomped out sometime around three to buy more alcohol and hadn't returned. Something must have happened to her. But he almost didn't care. He probably should have gone looking just in case, but then he'd be late for school. Besides, where would he start looking?

"The bus drivers all went on strike."

Jayden cocked his head, drawing his eyebrows together. "Strike? Why?"

"Dunno, guess they want more money. They're off for the whole week, which means no bus to school."

Jayden shrugged. "No big deal. I don't mind walking."

When they reached the front of the apartment complex, rain pelted down on the double glass doors. The sound was deafening.

"Still don't mind walking?" Roger raised his eyebrows and shot Jayden a teasing grin. "It's a good thing Mom agreed to drive me. You can ride with us, but you'll have to get your mom to pick you up. I've got a dentist visit this afternoon." Roger pulled the hood of his jacket over his head and darted outside to his mom's waiting car. Jayden followed suit.

The rain didn't let up all day. When the school bell rang that afternoon and Jayden joined the mob of students peering out at the driving rain, he decided to call Mum. Throughout the day he'd wondered if she'd made it home okay, but now his heart raced as her phone sent him to voice mail for the third time. What if something had happened to her? He should have gone looking. Dread settled in his stomach like a lead balloon. Where was she? He punched her number again.

"Hello?" Mum's voice was croaky and slurred.

Jayden breathed a sigh of relief.

"Mum, it's me. Where've you been?"

"Just asleep. Why?"

"The bus drivers are on strike and it's pouring with rain. Can you pick me up?"

"Sure, I'll come." She yawned. "Give me twenty minutes."

"Thanks." At least she wasn't still angry with him. He hadn't meant to upset her, just wake her up to what she was doing. Her drinking was turning into a major problem.

Jayden leaned against a wall and waited. Every few minutes he checked the time. Twenty minutes turned into an hour, and

Mum still wasn't there. His heart sank. All the other students had already gone, picked up by responsible parents who'd come on time. The school parking lot was empty except for one lone car.

One of the side doors to the school building opened and the janitor walked out. An aged man with a balding head, he walked slowly with a slight limp. Jayden had seen him around, cleaning the classrooms and hallways.

"Excuse me, son." The janitor stopped beside Jayden and spoke in a slow Texan drawl. "Someone picking you up?"

Jayden nodded a little too quickly. "Yeah, my mum's coming."

"You sure?" The janitor raised his eyebrows. "It's getting awfully late. Can you call her?"

Jayden shuffled his feet and shrugged. "I can try again."

"You do that. There's a tornado watch out so you need to get home. I don't mind taking you if she's not coming."

Jayden dialed Mum's number again but she didn't answer. He couldn't stand out in the rain any longer waiting for his mother who more than likely wasn't going to show up. He'd never experienced a tornado before, but he'd read about funnel clouds and knew how dangerous they could be, and certainly didn't want to get caught in one. "I'll ride with you. Thank you, Mr. ... " Jayden quickly looked at the janitor's nametag. "Mr. Cummings." Jayden shoved his phone back into his pocket and followed Mr. Cummings to his car. "I really appreciate it. Thanks."

"We're all put here to help somebody in some way at some time." Mr. Cummings smiled at him warmly as he turned the key in the ignition. "That's what my mama always told me."

"Your mama sounds like a good woman."

"She was. The best a boy could ask for."

*Not like my mother. She couldn't even stay sober long enough to pick me up from school.* Jayden's eyes blurred with tears.

He turned his head and wiped his eyes before giving directions to the apartment. Upon arriving, he thanked the kindly old man for the ride and then trudged up the stairs.

Everything was just as he'd left it that morning. "Mum…" Jayden tiptoed through the empty apartment. He swallowed the lump in his throat.

He went back out into the hallway and knocked on Roger's door.

Roger's six-year-old sister, Reye Beth, opened the door. She looked up at him with her dark brown eyes. "Roger can't talk. The dentist hurt him real bad." Her voice was sing-songy and kind of cute.

"Reye, who are you blabbing to?" Roger's mother called from the kitchen. She stuck her head around the corner and smiled at Jayden. With her brown hair and warm personality, she reminded him a little of Tessa. "Oh, Jay, I've been looking for you. I'm sorry about your mother."

"What about my mum?"

"Come in here and sit down."

Jayden followed Reye Beth as she skipped ahead of him into the brightly lit kitchen that smelled of garlic and spices. A pot bubbled away on the stove. Roger sat at the table with his head resting on his arms. He lifted his head and gave Jayden a wave before flopping it back down.

"See," Reye Beth said, pointing at Roger. "The dentist pulled out all his teeth and now he can't talk."

"Reye, will you stop it?" Roger's mother playfully swatted her with her free hand. "Roger only had one tooth pulled, and he can still talk just fine. He'll be back to normal in no time."

Jayden took a seat and tried to quell the concern growing inside him. *What happened to Mum?*

Roger's mother gave the pot a final stir, wiped her hands on her apron, then sat beside him. She lowered her voice. "Jay, a police officer came by about an hour or so ago."

Jayden's eyes widened.

"Your mom's been arrested for drunk driving. They found her not far from the school, slumped over the steering wheel of her car." Roger's mother squeezed his hand. "I'm really sorry, honey. You're welcome to stay here until she's released."

Jayden blinked back tears. He didn't know if he was angry with his mother or just disappointed and sad. Maybe he was all three.

"Thank you, Mrs. Jenkins, but I should be okay."

"Well, stay for dinner at least."

Jayden ate the spaghetti set before him, but didn't really taste it. He went back to the apartment and crawled into bed. Curled up in a ball, he tried to sleep, but visions of Mum in a jail cell kept flashing through his mind. If only it was all a nightmare he'd wake up from.

Sometime through the night he fell asleep. When he awoke the next morning, Mum was curled up on the couch snoring. Black make-up stained her face, and her hair was matted and untidy. He sighed. He couldn't leave her, not the way she was. Who knew what would happen to her if he did? At least Dad had Tessa, but if he left Mum, she'd have nobody. He wanted to be angry with her, but instead, a wave of pity flowed through him. He pulled a spare blanket out of the laundry room and placed it over her. Sighing heavily, he dragged himself into the kitchen to make breakfast. He wouldn't be going to school today.

KATHRYN RUSHED in one evening a couple of weeks later as Jayden was watching television and announced they had to pack.

Jayden's eyes narrowed. Since the drunk driving episode, she hadn't been drinking as much and he was beginning to hope that everything was settling down. But now? What had she done this time? His shoulders slumped. "Why do we need to pack? Did you lose your job?"

"No, we just can't stay here anymore."

He let out an annoyed sigh. "Why not?"

"I don't need an interrogation from you." She snapped open her gold cigarette case, pulling a cigarette out. "Just pack your bags and be ready to go in the morning."

"Where are we going this time?"

"Not sure." His mother flicked her cigarette lighter and lit up, took a deep drag and then blew a cloud of smoke out the side of her mouth.

"What do you mean you don't know?" Jayden jolted upright. "How can you expect me to pack up and leave, and not know where we're going? I'd rather go back home to Dad."

She moved quickly, slapping him on the face, making it smart. "Don't you ever talk to me like that, Jay."

Jayden's eyes widened. He felt his face. How dare she hit him! He glared at her.

"I'm not going."

"You are, and you'll go and pack. Now." She pointed in the direction of his room.

Jayden shook his head, fixing his eyes on her as he strode past. He went to his room and pulled all his belongings out of his closet and chucked them into a bag before collapsing on his bed, his chest heaving.

His mind swirled. Another move. But if he were honest, he didn't really like it here. Maybe it wouldn't be such a bad thing to move again. Get away from his so called friends and not feel pressured to party. He let out a heavy sigh and closed his eyes.

EARLY THE FOLLOWING MORNING, a truck came and took away all their furniture; it wasn't going with them. Jayden grimaced as they stepped outside with their bags. Instead of the sleek black convertible, an old Toyota Camry sat in their parking spot.

Jayden paused, bag in hand. "What happened to the car, Mum?"

"Sold it." His mother unlocked the Camry and opened the trunk.

"Have we got any money left?" Jayden stood to her side, his eyes fixed on her.

"Not your problem."

Jayden humphed as he threw his bags into the trunk and slammed it shut. *Yes, it is.*

"We'll be okay. Trust me." She gave him a reassuring smile as she slid into the driver's seat.

Jayden let out a resigned sigh. He didn't have much choice. "So which way are we headed?"

She shrugged. "North, I guess."

"It's winter. We'll freeze."

"It'll be an adventure." She shot him a playful grin.

"Where will we spend Christmas?"

She shrugged. "I don't know. Maybe we can find some snow and have a white Christmas." She turned the key and the car spluttered to life.

Catching sight of Roger coming down the stairs, Jayden slumped in his seat and pulled his cap over his face. At least Roger's focus was on his phone, and not on the crapped out car driving out of the parking lot.

# CHAPTER 15

*K*athryn and Jayden drove for two weeks. Jayden treated it like a vacation—he really had no choice. They stopped somewhere just north of Dallas and bought warmer clothing. And snow chains. At the first sight of snow, he couldn't help but remember the day he'd left Dad and Tessa on the ski trip in New Zealand and disappeared with Mum. She'd promised so much, and now here they were, all their worldly belongings stuffed into this run down old car, heading to who knew where. He should never have left Australia, but it was too late now. Mum needed him, and besides, it was kind of an adventure.

Sitting in the car for hours on end gave him plenty of time to think, and the question as to why Mum had left in the first place grew in his mind. Dad had never given him a definite reason, and Mum had never talked about it. He remembered the day she left. The disbelief when Dad said she'd gone and wasn't coming back. *How could she have done that?* **Why** *did she* *do it?* The emptiness he'd felt in the following days and weeks. And months. Okay, she'd never been a really fun type of mum. In fact, she often preferred reading magazines instead of playing with him when he was younger, and she'd never seemed that interested in what he was doing as he got older, but she was still his mum. And mums were supposed to love their kids, weren't they? Not abandon them. He needed to know why she left him.

Somewhere along the road, after several days of steeling himself, he turned from the never-ending road and looked at her. "Mum, can I ask you something?"

She glanced at him, her head tilted. "Of course. What is it?"

"Why did you leave?"

His gaze remained steady on her while he waited for an answer.

Her hands froze on the wheel, and her lower lip twitched.

"Wha...what makes you ask that?" Her voice, thin and shaky, was barely audible.

"I'd just like to know. That's all."

Her shoulders slumped as her grip on the wheel slowly eased. "I was bored. Bored with life." Her voice was quiet. Subdued.

"But you had me. Did I bore you?" Jayden's eyes narrowed as his heart began a free-fall.

She turned her head and reached out her hand. "Oh Jay, I didn't mean it like that." She gave him puppy dog eyes before turning her attention back to the road. "I wasn't cut out to be a housewife. I probably should never have married your father." She paused, a wistful expression on her face, as if she were remembering. "He wanted me to be something I wasn't, and when I met Luke, I knew that was the chance I'd been waiting for, and I took it." She glanced at him. "And I thought you'd be better off with your dad than with me." Her eyes glistened. "But I was wrong, Jay. I missed you. I missed you like anything. The day I saw you at the Pro-Am just about killed me."

*Yeah right. You ignored me. Pretended you hadn't seen me.*

"I wanted to talk with you, but I couldn't." She gulped. "Luke... " She let out a sad sigh.

"What, Mum? What about Luke?"

She exhaled slowly, her arms sagging. "He didn't like children."

Jayden shook his head in disbelief. "You never told him, did you?"

Tears rolled down her cheeks. "No... " Her chest shuddered as she reached out her hand again. "I'm so sorry, Jay."

He pushed her hand away. He should never have let her back into his life. She was right all along. He was better off with Dad.

They sat in silence as the miles drifted by. Dad had still been sending emails, but they all said the same thing. *'Come home, we miss you.'* Jayden never read any further than that. Maybe he should. But if he did, he'd want to go back. Could he do that? Admit he'd been wrong? His stomach churned. He really owed Mum nothing. He should leave her, just like she'd left him. It'd serve her right. Dad would pay his fare. All Jayden had to do was call him. But if he did, it would all be over. Just like that. He stared ahead. *Could he do it?*

. . .

ON CHRISTMAS EVE, Kathryn and Jayden approached a small town in Montana not far from the Canadian border.

Kathryn pulled over in a vista point overlooking the town set in a valley between two mountains. Snow covered the ground and hung off the trees in icicles. Smoke rose from chimneys of the houses far below, drifting into the air, and beckoning them to come down and get warm. "Let's take a look, Jay."

"It's freezing." Jayden's teeth chattered as he pulled his jacket tighter and rubbed his gloved hands together. When he exhaled, his breath looked like smoke spiraling into the crisp air.

Kathryn wrapped her arms around him. "This will do, Jay. We'll find a nice warm place with a fire. It's the perfect place to spend Christmas."

"Hope so." Jayden couldn't stop his teeth from chattering and jumped back into the car, turning the heater up high.

The road into the town of Hunters Hollow snaked down the side of the mountain. A snowplow had been through recently and snow was piled up on either side. Jayden held his breath as Kathryn inched her way forward over the slippery sections and around the 'U' bends. When they reached the straight road at the bottom, he let out his breath.

Small cottages began to appear and grew closer together as they approached the town. A sign welcomed them. The main street was decorated for Christmas with colorful bunting crisscrossing the road, and a huge Christmas tree covered with brightly painted pine cones and baubles took pride of place in the town square. Although it was only mid-afternoon, lights began to flicker on, and the whole town looked like a winter wonderland.

"It's pretty, isn't it?" Mum's voice was the softest Jayden had heard it in a long time. She really was trying.

"Yeah, I guess. But where are we going to stay?" Mary and Joseph's story flashed through his mind. He didn't want to sleep in a barn.

"We'll find somewhere. Don't worry, Jay."

He raised his brow. He hadn't seen any place with a vacancy sign.

Mum continued driving slowly through the town. People wearing thick jackets and gloves scurried along the pavements, ducking in and out of the small shops lining the main street, buying last minute gifts for their families, Jayden assumed. If he was back home… but no, he couldn't allow his thoughts to wander. But he couldn't help but wonder what Dad and Tessa were doing. It was already Christmas morning in Brisbane.

Mum hit the brakes and the car skidded to a sudden stop in front of a run down hotel that had a 'Vacancy' sign out front. "There, I told you we'd find something." She smiled at him and chuckled. "Come on Jay, let's get warm."

Inside, an open fire roared, and Kathryn and Jayden headed straight for it, rubbing their hands together and standing as close as they could.

"Can I help you, Ma'am?" A large man with shoulders rounded like a bull called out from behind the desk at the entrance they'd raced past in their hurry to get to the fire.

Jayden glanced at his mother. *Does she have enough money?* Dread settled in his stomach. She'd been very cagey about how much she actually had left.

"Ah, yes." She walked to the desk and stood in front of the man. Jayden didn't like the way she'd swung her hips. What was she trying to do? "We…" she reached for Jayden and placed her hand on his shoulder, "we'd like a room for two nights please."

The man looked her up and down. "On yer way somewhere?"

Jayden was about to tell him to mind his own business when she spoke. "We might hang around awhile. Depends." She batted her eyelashes.

Jayden groaned. Why would Mum flirt with someone as ugly as him?

"I have a room on the top floor. In fact, two rooms, inter-connecting." He lifted his gaze from the desk. "I can let you have them both for the price of one." The man gave Mum a look that sent shivers down Jayden's spine.

"That would be perfect. Thank you, Mr.?"

"Call me Buck. And you are?" He cocked his head.

"Katy."

Jayden's brow shot up.

"And this is my son, Jay." She placed both her hands on his shoulders.

Buck nodded once and gave him a frosty look. Jayden's pulse raced. There was something about this man he didn't like.

"And how much will that be?" Mum reached for her purse.

"Fix me up later. I'll show you to your rooms."

"Thank you. That's very kind of you, Buck." Mum put on her sickly sweet voice. Jayden hated it.

He followed Mum and Buck up the three flights of threadbare stairs and gagged when he entered his room. The cigarette fumes at the apartment in Austin were nothing compared to the suffocating haze hanging in the air of this tiny room. He held his hand to his mouth and coughed.

"Sorry about that. Ventilation's died." Buck chuckled, but it wasn't a kind chuckle. It was a chuckle that conveyed malice. *What have I done to make him hate me?* Jayden's jaw tightened as he glared at Buck.

"And this here is the room for the lovely lady."

Jayden balled his hands as he fought the anger growing inside him.

Buck left after a while, and as soon as his heavy footsteps faded, Jayden raced into Mum's room. She was unpacking her bags and had started putting her clothes into the four-drawer wooden dresser beside the window.

"We can't stay here, Mum." Jayden kept his voice low but firm.

"Oh Jay." She reached out her hands. He ignored them. "It's only until we get ourselves sorted. It'll be okay, you'll see."

He glared at her. "Fine. Two days, that's all."

"I promise." She resumed unpacking. "How about we freshen up and then go down for dinner? Buck said they're having a Christmas Eve singalong around the fire."

"Sounds great." Jayden rolled his eyes. He couldn't be any more sarcastic if he tried.

The evening dragged. Mum drank too much and played up to Buck all night. It made Jayden sick. He snuck out just before ten o'clock, but instead of climbing the stairs to his suffocating room, he slipped out the side door and headed to town.

Not surprisingly, very few people were out. Freshly fallen

snow crunched under his feet as Jayden walked briskly along the pavement. He passed shops and cafés, all decorated for Christmas but now closed for business. But up ahead, a familiar Christmas carol sounded from a small church on his right.

He crossed the road carefully, not wanting to slip and fall, and sidled up to the window. The building itself reminded him of Gracepoint church back home, with its 'A'-framed gable and cross sitting on the apex. A whole range of people filled the pews. Elderly men and women, some holding hands, and young children who probably should have been in bed. But they all stood and sang. As the words of "Silent Night" reached his ears, tears sprang to his eyes. Last Christmas he and Dad and Tessa had gone to the Christmas Eve service with Tessa's parents. But instead of snow on the ground and heating inside to warm the congregation, fans had whirred at full speed to disperse the thick, sweltering air hanging inside the chapel. But the carols they'd sung were the very same ones being sung here.

A lump rose in his throat. Jayden shivered and lifted the collar of his jacket higher around his neck. He couldn't keep standing there. He had to go in or keep walking. He was just about to move on when a hand touched his shoulder. A kindly looking man about the same age as Dad stood beside him.

"Coming in, son? You'll freeze out here."

Jayden looked into the man's friendly eyes. It was tempting, that was for sure. He made up his mind, and followed the man inside. The warm air hit his face like a blast from an oven. He removed his jacket and hung it on a hook in the foyer. The man showed him to a seat in the back row and stood beside him as the carol continued. Jayden gulped and pushed back tears. If only it were Dad standing beside him.

The song changed. The man gave him a song sheet but he didn't need it. He knew the words to 'Oh Come, all ye Faithful.' Jayden joined in, at first just mouthing the words, but then singing them. Something inside pulled at his heart as he sang, and tears rolled down his cheeks. He quickly wiped them away with his hand, but they kept coming. The man gave him a handkerchief and placed his arm lightly on Jayden's shoulders.

What was he doing here? He should be back home with his own dad. *You're here now, son. I'm with you.* Jayden looked around. Where did that come from? Everyone was still singing. No-one had spoken to him. *I love you. You're precious to me.* Jayden gulped. It had to be God, speaking to him. He squeezed his eyes shut and swallowed. He didn't know what to do. The carol ended and everyone sat. He had to get out of here. Instead of taking his seat, Jayden slipped out of the end of the pew, grabbed his jacket and stepped outside. The blast of freezing air stung his face, but he was oblivious to it. His insides churned with a whirling jumble of memories, regrets and now the voice of God. He trudged back the way he came, trying to make sense of it all. But no sense came. His life was a mess, and now he had to sleep in that horrible room.

# CHAPTER 16

*J*ayden's mind was a-whirl when he woke the following morning. Had it all been a dream? Had he really walked down the street and found that church? Had that man really placed his hand on his shoulder and led him inside? *Did God really speak to me?* Jayden climbed out of bed and checked his pockets. The man's handkerchief was balled up inside one of them. It was real. It had happened. He sat on the edge of the bed and hung his head. *God, I don't know how to talk to you, but if you want to speak to me, I'm listening.* Nothing happened. But the words he'd heard last night played through his mind. *'I love you. You're precious to me.'* He swallowed and let out a slow breath. *God, I should know how to do this, but I don't, but I thank you for being with me. I could really do with a friend right now, so if you're up there, I wouldn't mind hearing from you.*

A thump sounded from the next room. He looked up. Had Mum fallen out of bed? The floorboards creaked, as if someone heavier than Mum was walking on them. His shoulders slumped. *Buck.* A sick feeling grew in his stomach. Already he'd grown to hate that man.

He lay back in bed and curled up, pulling the comforter tight around his neck to keep out the cold. It might be Christmas Day, but there was nothing joyous about it. Especially with Buck in it.

HE MUST HAVE FALLEN ASLEEP, because he woke sometime later to persistent knocking on his door. "Jay, wake up. It's breakfast time."

He drew in a breath and sat up. "Give me a minute." He climbed out of bed and pulled on some fresh clothes before opening the door.

"Merry Christmas, Jay." Mum gave him a huge hug. Her over-the top smile had returned.

"Merry Christmas, Mum." He couldn't summons any enthusiasm.

"Let's go down." She linked arms with him and pranced down the stairs as if she were a madam and he a gentleman. It made him sick.

Only two others ate breakfast in the dining area of the hotel. A middle-aged man and woman who nodded as he and Mum entered. At least Buck was nowhere in sight.

"Well, this is nice, isn't it, Jay?" She flashed another smile.

Jayden forced one in return.

Mum chatted non-stop, as if she were trying to cover up the fact that Buck had been in her room all night.

"Come to church with me?" He interrupted her.

She stopped mid-sentence. "I haven't set foot in a church for years, Jay. Besides, Buck has asked us to have lunch here with him."

*Great.* Jayden steadied his breathing. He could get really angry if he wasn't careful. "There's plenty of time before lunch." He checked his watch. "The service starts in half an hour."

"You go if you want, Jay, I might catch up on some sleep." She yawned.

"Mum, it's Christmas." Tears welled in his eyes. How could she be so thoughtless?

She reached out and touched his wrist. "I'm sorry, Jay. I'll make it up to you." Her expression brightened. "But at least we've got a place to stay for as long as we want."

Jayden's eyes narrowed. "What do you mean?"

"Buck's got a cottage on the edge of town we can stay in if I work here for free."

Jayden glanced at the man and woman before leaning closer. "I don't like the sound of that. Can't we find somewhere for ourselves?"

"It'll help us out for a while, Jay." She squeezed his hand, holding his gaze. An embarrassed look grew on her face. "Besides, we don't have enough money for anything else."

"What happened to the money, Mum?" He couldn't believe he was hearing this. The condo, the boat, the fancy car, the private plane—all gone. What had she done? She hadn't even given him a Christmas present.

She gave a half shrug, her eyes moistening. Squeezing his hand tighter, she leaned closer and lowered her voice. "You don't know what it's been like, Jay." Her voice caught in her throat. "I've been so lonely since Luke left. And I may have ... " she sniffed and turned her head away, holding her free hand to her nose.

"Done what, Mum?" Jayden drew his eyebrows together and stared at her. Did he really want to find out?

She sniffed again and turned her head slowly. She plucked at a piece of fluff on her sleeve before raising her eyes. "I may have ... gambled it."

Jayden's eyes widened. He ripped his hand away from hers. How could she have gambled all their money? *How dare she?* "I'm out of here, Mum. Sorry." Tears stung his eyes as he pushed his chair back and raced for the exit.

Jayden felt, rather than saw, Buck's eyes on him. *She's all yours, Buck. I'm outta here.*

His heart thumped as he entered the street. He looked both ways. The only place he knew was the church, and that was to the left. But did he want to go back there? To be pitied by people who wouldn't understand? People in normal families sitting together singing Christmas carols, looking forward to a big Christmas dinner in houses that were warm and safe, having hugged and kissed each other as they opened lovingly wrapped presents this morning? No, he couldn't go there. He turned and headed the other way.

Snow fell lightly as he walked, and by late morning, Jayden had reached the other end of town. He couldn't keep walking. His feet, cold and numb, felt like they didn't belong to him and would fall off at any second. Aromas of roast Christmas dinners wafted out of all the houses he passed, tantalizing his taste buds. With very little money and nowhere specific to go, he had no real plan. Stopping outside a derelict building, he peered through the boarded up, dirty windows. It had once been a shop of some sort, a café, perhaps? He could hang out in there for a while. A lump formed in his throat. What was he thinking? How could he do that, especially in this weather? But what option did he have? He knew no-one, apart from Mum. And Buck. And maybe that man at church last night.

He blinked back tears as the lump rose higher in his throat. Sliding to the ground, he buried his head in his hands and burst into tears. He'd never felt so alone in all his life. A nauseating feeling grew in his stomach. He had no choice—he had to go back to Mum. And Buck.

Picking himself up off the ground, he trudged back to the hotel and peered inside the window. Unlike the other more salubrious establishments in town that he'd passed on his way back, 'Hunters Hollow Hotel' had few Christmas decorations, and the few that were up were gaudy and old. Even the Christmas tree was small and fake, just a token effort. Several people sat in the dining room finishing their lunch, but not Mum. He slipped inside and up the stairs, his heart pounding. Buck was nowhere to be seen, but what if he ran into him? He reached the top floor safely and paused outside Mum's door. Silence. He knocked tentatively.

"Jay, is that you?" Her sleepy voice called out.

He opened the door and peeked in. Mum looked terrible. Her make-up had run down her face and her eyes were red and swollen. She threw back the covers and held out her arms.

"Jay, I'm sorry. Come here."

Jayden drew in a slow breath. How pitiful she looked. So different to the trendy, well-dressed woman who'd whisked him away from Dad and Tessa only months before. He stepped slowly towards her. What would life be like in this town with a broke mother and a brute of a man lurking around? He tried to push down the apprehension growing deep inside him. How could he leave her now? *God, I have no idea what's ahead, but please be with me.*

THAT AFTERNOON, after Mum had showered and made herself presentable, she and Jayden took a drive to check out the cottage. Although only two miles out of town, it seemed to him they were driving for hours. The road wound up a valley that narrowed with each corner. In some places snow blocked their way. Jayden got out and shoveled it off the road. They only passed two other houses; one abandoned, but outside the other, a number of cars were parked. He breathed a sigh of relief—at least they'd have neighbors.

As they rounded yet another corner, the cottage came into view. His heart fell. If the outside was anything to go by, the inside would be a mess. The yard was littered with rusting farm equipment and old car tires. A derelict barn sat to the right of the one-storey cottage. Paint was peeling off the outside walls, and the bushes surrounding it were all over-grown and heavy with snow.

He slumped in his seat, folding his arms. "Don't like the look of this."

Mum remained silent, her eyes fixed on the cottage. After several seconds, she turned to him. "I don't either Jay, but we don't have a choice."

"I'm not going in."

"Yes, you are."

He shook his head. "How can you even consider living in this run-down hovel?"

She shrugged, her lip quivering. "Jay, please don't talk to me like that." She sniffed, sounding like she was about to cry. "I'm sorry, I really am." She reached her hand out to him. "We'll stay just until I make some money. Okay?"

Jayden let out a resigned sigh and opened the car door. The gate wouldn't budge when he tried to move it—snow was piled up on both sides. He took the shovel from the trunk and started shoveling.

A few minutes later, he pushed the gate open and led the way up the stairs and onto the porch. "Have you got the key?"

Mum nodded and handed it to him.

He inserted the key into the lock and opened the door. At least it had furniture, but the smell of dust and stale urine made him gag. He held his hand to his nose.

"We can clean it." Mum placed her arm on his shoulder as tears streamed down her cheeks.

Jayden drew in a breath. He knew who'd be doing the cleaning. As they wandered through the house, he couldn't believe his mother would lower herself to live in a place like this.

"We'll come back tomorrow and start cleaning. Buck said he'll chop wood for us. It'll be okay." She stood, a blank look on her face. She'd resigned herself to living here, and involving Buck in their lives.

Jayden couldn't believe it. The heavy weight grew in his stomach.

.   .   .

JAYDEN CLEANED the cottage with a token effort from Kathryn. It took all day, but by the time he'd finished, it looked almost inhabitable. Buck turned up mid-morning with a load of wood and lit the fire. Jayden kept his distance. He didn't like the way the man seemed to think he already owned his mother.

The first night in the cottage, Jayden lay in his bed and put on some music. At least the cottage had electricity even if it didn't have Internet or phone. He put his earphones in and tried to pretend he was anywhere other than here. Buck had stayed and was with Mum. Seemed that was payment for the cottage and the job.

## CHAPTER 17

"*A*migos, la bienvenida a Ecuador!" Elliott greeted as Ben and Tessa quickly ducked through body scans and came towards him at Guayaquil's International Airport.

"Let me guess," Tessa said, hugging him tightly. "Friends, welcome to Ecuador."

"Right on," Elliott said. "You must have been studying."

"We've been trying." Ben put his hand forward and shook Elliott's hand. "So far, I've managed hola, buenos días, adiós, si, gracias, and of course amigo, but everyone knows that."

"I didn't get much further." Tessa pulled a face.

Elliott laughed. "At least it's a start. I've learned to speak it quite well, actually, but there's still some room for improvement. A few of the locals in Daule, where the mission grounds are, know a bit of English, sort of broken, but they'll understand you quite well."

Tessa took a step back to take a good look at her younger brother. The last time she'd seen him was when he'd flown back for their wedding, just over a year ago. He'd slimmed down, but packed on more muscle, and his skin was lightly tanned. His smile was still bright and his eyes sparkled with purpose. Being on mission was doing him good.

"Everything okay, Tess?" Elliott asked. "You're staring at me like I've turned into a ghost."

"Oh, no," Tessa laughed. "It's just that you look a bit different."

"Yeah, I guess Ecuador will do that to you. Who knows? By the time you two leave, you'll probably look and feel different too." Elliott picked up one of her suitcases and led the way outside to where his red jeep was waiting.

Tessa was used to warm weather, but she gagged at the hot humid air that hit her as they left the terminal.

"Most days are like this, sis. You'll get used to it." Elliott flashed her a cheeky smile. "Even when the sun isn't shining, it's still hot, being so close to the equator. And it can start pouring anytime without warning, but don't worry, it's usually just a gentle rain, not huge thunderstorms."

"Glad to hear it. I see you haven't slowed down talking at all." She ducked in case Elliott decided to give her a playful whack.

With their luggage in the back seat of the jeep, the three rode in the front with Tessa squeezed in between Elliott and Ben. The air conditioner wasn't working, and in its place a mobile radio kit had been installed. "So I can keep in touch with the folks back at the grounds. It operates just like an intercom system. If something goes wrong or if there's an emergency while we're apart, I can call them or they can call me."

"I'd prefer air-con." Tessa fanned herself and took a sip of water.

Elliott shrugged. "A luxury we can't afford. Sorry." He glanced at Tessa as he pulled onto a busy highway. "I was quite surprised to hear from you. But you know, we'd been praying for extra volunteers, so I see it as an answer to prayer."

Ben and Tessa looked at one another. Should they tell him the real reason they'd decided to come? Eleanor had left it to them to tell Elliott about Jayden leaving. "I guess Jayden wanted to stay in Australia and enjoy Mum's good cooking." He gave a small chuckle. "How is he?"

They'd have to tell him. Tessa gulped as Ben squeezed her hand. "Well, truth be told, he's actually the reason we decided to get away and spend some time here." She paused and let out a slow breath. "Jayden ran away and is living with his mother."

"No! He didn't?" Elliott looked at her with eyes as wide as golf balls.

Tessa nodded. "Unfortunately, he did. We've done every-thing we could to get him back, but nothing's worked. Seems he's happy in the States with her, for the moment at least, so we thought a change of scenery would do us good. Get our mind off him for a while. Hopefully being here will help us do that. Plus we can help you."

Elliott gestured at the car in front that turned without indi-cating before glancing back at Tessa. "Why did he leave? I hope he wasn't still upset with me."

"No, you had nothing to do with it." Ben leaned forward and cleared his throat. "It's mainly Kathryn's doing, but I do accept some of the blame. I don't think I was understanding enough."

Tessa squeezed Ben's hand.

"I'm sorry to hear that, Ben. He's a good kid, and God's working on him. I'm sure he'll come back in time. I'll be sure to pray for him." Elliott's voice was full of concern and compassion. He remained silent for a few seconds, as if he were praying for Jayden right then and there. "But in the meantime, I'm glad you're here—I'm sure it'll do you both good."

Tessa let out a slow sigh. "We hope so."

They soon left the noisy, but vibrant and sprawling city of Guayaquil behind. The downtown high-rises disappeared into the rearview distance, and hillsides covered in colourful shantytowns rose up around them. After about an hour, they turned off the well-paved highway onto a narrow dirt road full of ruts and dried mud patches. Swampy meadows of green grass spread out on either side of the dirt road, with patches of leafy Tagua palms standing nearly forty feet tall, giving it a real tropical feel.

The mission was spread out on both sides of a dirty brown tributary of water that flowed into the larger Daule River. Several children were running around, laughing and playing with plastic balls when Elliott's jeep came to a stop. Tessa waved to them, and they waved back, staring and smiling shyly.

"Mayta, Santiago, Juan," Elliott said, calling their names. After talking to them in Spanish, they shed their shyness and ran up to shake hands with Ben and Tessa. The children's eyes lit up when Ben took a pack of gum out of his pocket and gave them each a piece.

"We work on both sides of the water," Elliott said. "The living quarters are mostly over here, but on the other side

CHAPTER 17 | 121

we've built a church and we just finished building a school for the mission. There's still some things that need to be completed though, like the interior and the playground, but most of the heavy-duty work is done. We also keep our supplies and the plane over there in the storage building."

"How do you get across?" Ben asked.

"There used to be a bridge, but every time the river flooded, it got damaged, so we stopped repairing it." Elliott pointed to three objects that looked like rafts floating on top of the water, tied to stakes in the ground. "Now we use flatboats to go across."

The doors of one of the houses opened, and a broad, tawny-skinned woman with the same coloured hair and eyes came out. "Elliott, you're back." She spoke in English but with a strong Spanish accent.

"Hello, Maria. I've brought our new workers."

"I can see that. Welcome, Ben. Welcome, Tessa." Maria greeted Ben and Tessa in turn with a warm hug and kiss. "Your brother has told me many good things about you, so I'm glad that we get to meet at last. Come, let me show you to your lodgings."

# CHAPTER 18

essa held Ben's hand as they followed Maria to a small house towards the edge of the village. Perched on stilts and made of cane, it reminded Tessa of one of the Three Little Pigs' houses, and she wondered how safe it was.

Maria must have seen the look of concern on Tessa's face. "Don't worry, Tessa. It's perfectly safe." She chuckled as she lumbered up the rickety stairs. "See, it's fine."

Tessa sucked in a breath and followed her up. The house was sparsely furnished, with just a bedroom, a bathroom, and a living room which also doubled as a kitchen and dining area. Although the furnishings were simple, the colours of the floor rugs, cushions and wall hangings were so vibrant they took Tessa's breath away.

"It's lovely. Thank you." Tessa's heart expanded at the simple joy flowing from the dark-haired woman's face as she stood there expectantly with her hands clutched in front of her.

"It doesn't have all the amenities like back home," Elliott said, joining them with a handful of luggage, "but you get used to it. The people more than make up for what the country lacks in resources. They're warm and friendly for the most part, and eager to help."

"I can see that already." Tessa smiled again at Maria and then sniffed the air. A strong, spicy aroma wafted through the house. "What smells so good?"

"Your dinner." Elliott crossed the floor to the kitchen and lifted the lid of the earthenware pot sitting on the simple two-burner stove. "Maria cooked it for you."

Maria glanced at her hands coyly. "I thought you'd be tired from your long flight. It's *guatita*, a traditional Ecuadorian stew made with beef tripe, potatoes and peanut sauce."

Tessa raised her eyebrows but quickly lowered them. *Tripe?*

"I'm pretty sure you'll love it," Elliott said, stepping back and placing his arm lightly on Maria's shoulder. "I've come to love all different kinds of Ecuadorian foods since I've been here, and *guatita* is still one of my favourite dishes. And Maria's the best cook."

A flush crept up the woman's face.

"Well, it certainly smells wonderful," Ben said. "We haven't eaten since lunch on the plane, so I'm quite hungry."

"Thank you, Maria." Tessa stepped forward and squeezed her hand. "We appreciate your thoughtfulness."

"My pleasure. And thank you again for coming." The woman's white teeth sparkled as a smile lit up her face. "If you need anything else to get settled in, just let me know." She waved as she and Elliott disappeared down the stairs.

"I THINK I'm going to like it here, Ben. What do you think?" Tessa asked as she began placing her clothes into the single closet in the bedroom.

"I think I'm going to like it very much." As Ben slipped his arms around her from behind and ran his lips softly along her neck, her knees weakened.

"Ben!"

"What?"

His kisses sent tingles down her spine. She laughed as she turned around and gazed into his eyes. "Have you forgotten where we are?"

"No, I haven't. We're in our bedroom."

She shook her head but a smile danced on her lips.

"I just wanted to let you know how much I love you, that's all."

"Oh Ben."

Her whole body melted as his lips brushed softly against hers.

SOON AFTER, they drifted into the kitchen and sat down to Maria's *guatita*. "I think I could get used to this. Even with the tripe." Tessa chuckled before taking another mouthful.

"This was a great idea, Tess. Just being away from home and all the memories has already made a difference."

"I can tell." She gave him a playful smile, but then his

expression changed.

"But I still can't help thinking about what Jayden's doing, especially now Neil's told us he's in Texas."

She sighed and reached for his hand. "God's with him, Ben. We've just got to leave Jayden in His care."

Ben let out a deep breath. "I know. But I've checked the distance between Ecuador and Texas. We're not that far away from him now. Maybe we should try to see him."

"We can try. You never know, he might be ready to see us."

Footsteps sounded on the steps, followed by a soft knock. "Tess, Ben, can I come in?"

"Yes, Elliott, come in. We're just finishing dinner." Tessa stood and carried the dishes to the sink.

Elliott joined her in the kitchen. "Enjoy it?" He ran a finger around the edge of the bowl and licked it.

She slapped his hand playfully. "What would Mum say?"

Elliott shrugged, flashing her a cheeky grin.

"But yes. It was just what we needed. I'll have to ask Maria to show me how to make it."

"Still can't cook, hey sis?"

Tessa was about to whack him with the dish towel when Ben joined them.

"She can cook better than me." Ben came up behind Tessa and rubbed her arms, sending goose-bumps down her arms. She hoped Elliott hadn't noticed.

"Would you like to meet the others before it gets dark? They'd like to meet you." Elliott leaned back on the kitchen counter, crossing his legs at the ankle.

Tessa twisted her head so she could see Ben. "Shall we?"

"Why not? Lead the way, Elliott. The dishes can wait."

. . .

ELLIOTT TOOK them around the mission grounds and introduced them to the other workers. Four were non-Ecuadorian. Trevor and Robert Lolarossi were American brothers in their mid-twenties who'd both attended mission school with Elliott in California. Larry and Penny Mykal were an older couple from Toronto, Canada. They'd been involved in mission work for most of their lives and were about the ages of Tessa's parents. They welcomed Ben and Tessa as if they were welcoming their own children.

Ben accompanied the men on one of the flatboats across the river to inspect the construction work. As Tessa watched him leave, she couldn't help but wonder how her accountant husband would fit in.

Meanwhile, Tessa sat down with Penny over a cup of tea while Penny gave her advice on how best to deal with bugs, how not to get sick in the constant heat and humidity, and how they managed to get by with washing their clothes by hand.

As she listened to the short, grey-haired woman talk with such enthusiasm about life on the mission, Tessa began to realise the extent of the sacrifices Penny and Larry had made to live here, and just how many of the everyday things that she took for granted, Penny had done without for most of her adult life.

"You sound like you love it here." Tessa gave Penny a warm smile.

"Yes, we both do, despite everything." She let out a small

chuckle. "We've been in a lot worse places than here, believe me!"

"Where have you been?" Tessa took a cookie off the plate.

"Oh, we've spent time in Ethiopia, Delhi, Seoul, our own home of Toronto, Salvador, Rio, and now here in Daule."

Tessa's eyes widened. "Wow! That's amazing."

"I guess so, but we've been on mission most of our lives. Larry and I met on a youth mission trip to Cambodia when we were in our early twenties. That trip changed us both so much that we decided to become missionaries instead of pursuing our original careers."

Tess sipped her tea. "What careers did you have?"

"Well, I'm a registered nurse, and Larry's an architect."

"I can see why you'd both be in demand on the mission field, but you must have had some challenging experiences."

Penny chuckled, her eyes lighting up. "Well, yes, you could say that. We've had a few challenges along the way. Maybe one day I'll tell you about some of them." She glanced up as footsteps sounded on the porch. Larry entered, followed by Ben.

Tessa had thought Ben tall, but Larry stood almost a foot taller, the top of his balding head just missing the bamboo ceiling by a whisker.

"So, what have you two been chatting about?" Larry leaned down and kissed Penny on the cheek.

Penny's eyes sparkled. "Wouldn't you like to know?"

Tessa swallowed the lump in her throat as she caught Ben's eye. Was he thinking the same as her? Would they still be in love like that when they were this couple's age?

"Probably just women's business." Larry winked at Ben. "Would you like a drink?"

"Thanks, that'd be great." Ben smiled and then joined Tessa on the couch, resting his arm behind her, twiddling a lock of her hair in his fingers. How long since he'd been this relaxed? It warmed her heart and confirmed they'd made the right decision.

# CHAPTER 19

*T*he following morning, it took Tessa a few moments to remember she was in Ecuador, not Brisbane. Lying in bed with her eyes closed, she breathed in the fresh mountain air wafting in through the thin curtains and relaxed. Bindy and Sparky weren't wagging their tails, waiting to be fed and walked. No vet clinic or city office to rush off to. Such a great feeling, being here with a changed Ben. Tessa lurched forward. *Ben.* He was meant to be flying to a remote area in a tiny plane this morning. Her heart raced as she turned her head. He was already gone.

She jumped out of bed, threw on a light robe and opened the door just in time to see the plane taxiing down the patch of dirt that was the runway on the other side of the river. She waved frantically until the plane disappeared into the early morning mist.

"They probably won't be back until noon." Elliott had taken the steps two at a time and joined her. "There's only space for two in the cockpit, otherwise you could have gone too." Elliott planted a kiss on her cheek. "Maybe you can go next time."

Tessa pulled back, shaking her head. "No way—you won't get me in a tiny plane like that!"

"Oh, come on, sis. Don't be a wuss." There was a glint of a tease in Elliott's eyes before his expression grew serious. "Trust me, nothing beats the exhilaration of soaring above the clouds and gazing down on huge mountains from a small plane, especially when you're doing it for a good reason."

"I'll think about it." Tessa shifted her gaze back to the mountains. The sun was just breaking the horizon, dispersing the mist and shedding light over the entire valley. "This is so beautiful, Elliott. I could sit and look at it all day, but that's not what I'm here for." She turned her head. "So what have you got planned for me today?"

"If you'd like, you could help Penny with her medical rounds, and then when Ben gets back, you can both help with building the playground for the school."

Tessa smiled at him. "Sounds great."

SHORTLY AFTER, Tessa joined Penny in her kitchen where she was busy collecting pill bottles, medicine droppers and syringes. "We need to re-use most of the equipment," Penny said as she placed the droppers and syringes into a bucket of boiling water.

Tessa raised an eyebrow.

"Supplies are very limited."

"Oh." *Of course they would be.* Tessa gulped as she thought about all the supplies they had sitting on the shelves at the vet clinic.

The morning sun warmed Tessa's skin as she and Penny set out to visit their first patient—a mother whose baby had been running a fever for the past ten days. Nearly all of the locals were out and the mission bustled with their chatter and the laughter of children. Half of the men and some of the young women were on the other side of the river with Elliott, Larry, and Robert, setting up desks and bookshelves and putting the final touches on the interior of the school building. The other men had gone off to work in the surrounding rice farms. The older women washed clothes on the edge of the river, beating them out on large flat rocks before hanging the wet clothes out to dry on rope stretched between the trees.

They all seemed happy. So different to back home where hardly anyone smiled as they went about their daily business. Here, an atmosphere of community permeated the entire mission ground. Young children to wizened grandparents living and working together, happily.

Several of the locals came up to Tessa and shyly introduced themselves, telling her in broken English how glad they were to have her and Ben with them. Despite the language barrier, Tessa felt she already belonged.

As Penny made her rounds, Tessa helped by handing her the supplies she needed and making friends with the children she encountered. She soon lost track of how many chocolate bars she handed out to their great delight. For the most part, though, Tessa observed as Penny administered shots, squeezed out drops, changed bandages, handed out pills, and applied medicinal salves and ointments. Penny explained things to

Tessa as she went along, so that next time she'd be able to participate more.

After the last patient for the day had been seen, they strolled back to Penny's house for lunch.

"I really enjoyed this morning, Penny, although it was kind of strange..."

Penny turned to her with a puzzled look on her face. "Strange? In what way?"

"Well, usually I'd be at work at a clinic... a vet clinic."

Penny's eyes widened. "Why didn't you tell me?"

"I work with animals, not people." Tessa chuckled. "Just a slight difference." She blew some stray hair off her face. "I thought I worked hard then, but after this morning, I'm not sure." She stifled a yawn.

"It takes time to get used to the heat. And you're probably still jet-lagged." Penny gave her an understanding smile as she opened the front door and turned the fans on. "Let me make some lunch and then maybe you should take a short nap before helping with the playground. You don't want to burn out on your first day."

"Sounds divine." Tessa stifled another yawn.


MID-AFTERNOON, Ben and Trevor returned in the plane. Ben waved as he weaved his way through the muddy plot of land beside the school building to where Tessa and the others were assembling the equipment for the playground.

Tessa brushed the mud off her hands before letting Ben hug and kiss her. She'd never seen him so animated.

Ben brushed back damp, sweaty hair from her forehead.

"We had the most remarkable time. It wasn't only the breath-taking sights, but the village was so appreciative of the supplies we delivered to them. You should have seen their faces. They couldn't stop thanking God and us enough. I haven't had such a good feeling about something I've done in the longest time."

She held him at arm's length before pulling him close and returning his hug. Yes, this was the Ben she knew. Only a few short weeks ago, he'd been depressed, distraught, and distracted over the situation with Jayden. His face, which had been heavy with anxiety and worry, was now full of life. Jayden still hadn't returned, but at least the real Ben was back.

# CHAPTER 20

O ver the following weeks, Ben and Tessa worked alongside Elliott and the others in laying the wooden floor of the school building, assembling desks and installing chalkboards. They also worked on the playground construction. Tessa loved watching Ben work. Although more at home with spreadsheets and figures, he hammered and sawed, dug and shoveled, and came home each night complaining about blisters and sunburn, but he was happier than Tessa had ever seen him.

But Jayden was never far from their thoughts. Each night Ben and Tessa prayed for him. They prayed for his safety, and pleaded with God to continue knocking on the door of his heart. And they never ceased praying for his return.

Every morning, Ben checked his emails on the mission's computer. Occasionally there'd be an email from Neil, but never one from Jayden. One morning Ben came back with a worried look on his face.

"Is there news?" Tessa's heart went into freefall as she immediately imagined the worst. She grabbed Ben's hand as he sat beside her at the table and peered into his eyes.

He sighed. "Not really. Just an email from Neil."

She raised a brow. "What did he say?"

"It's what he didn't say that's concerning me." He paused and met Tessa's gaze. "I think something's happened to Jayden he's not telling us."

"Like what?"

Ben sighed deeply. "I don't know. It's just a feeling."

She held Ben's gaze and tried to push the negative thoughts she'd had to the back of her mind, but she couldn't help wondering what might have happened.

"Do you think he's hurt? Or in danger?"

"I said I don't know. Normally Neil says that Jayden's having a ball over there, but this time all he said was that Jayden was okay." Ben paused, drawing in a deep breath. "Maybe I'm reading too much into it."

"Can you ask Neil?"

"I did, but I'm not expecting him to let on."

Silence filled the air for several seconds.

"I think we should try to see him."

Tessa nodded, tears pricking her eyes. "Yes, we should."

"Come on you two love birds. Break's over." Elliott stood at the end of the table with his arms folded, an amused look on his face.

Ben squeezed her hand. "Just the person we wanted to see..."

After Ben explained what had happened, Elliott was only too happy to give them as long as they needed. Ben booked seats on the first flight he could get from Guayaquil to Austin, Texas. They'd leave on Monday morning, the day after tomorrow.

THAT SUNDAY, everyone living on the mission grounds and a few others living nearby, gathered together in the church building for worship and preaching like they did every Sunday.

The only musical instruments the church had was Trevor's guitar, which he played expertly, and a pair of tambourines that Penny and one of the locals shook in time to the beat. A wooden crate, emptied of its store of oranges, served as a drum which nine-year old Santiago banged on with fervour. Everyone joined in singing the mixture of English and Spanish songs. Ben and Tessa had quickly learned the words to the English songs. They listened when the Spanish ones were sung, understanding a few words here and there.

Tessa hummed along, but tears pricked her eyes when Maria stood and began singing "Amazing Grace" unaccompanied in Spanish. She squeezed Ben's hand and closed her eyes. *Lord, please let Jayden know your amazing grace. Be with us as we go to him, and let his heart not only be open to us, but to you also, dear Lord.* Although weighed down by thoughts of Jayden, God's presence was real and Tessa was comforted by the knowledge that he cared more for Jayden than either she or Ben ever could, and they could trust him to do whatever was necessary to bring Jayden to salvation. And home.

Larry had been scheduled to preach, but at the last moment had taken ill. Tessa smiled as Elliott stood and walked to the front. When he'd spoken to the youth group at Gracepointe

Church several years ago, his preaching had been very ordinary. She expected him now to speak God's word with passion and skill. He'd grown in maturity, both as a man and as a Christian, and her heart swelled with pride as Elliott smiled warmly at the eager faces waiting for a message from God.

She wished she knew what he was saying, but when he finished and the familiar tune of "What a friend we have in Jesus" began to play, she smiled. *Yes, Lord, what a privilege it is to carry everything to you in prayer.*

MONDAY MORNING CAME QUICKLY, and before they knew it, Ben and Tessa were in the air flying towards Texas with hope in their hearts. Neil had given them the last address he had for Jayden, and they gave this to the taxi driver at the airport. Jayden's ninety days were up, and it was possible, no probable, that he and Kathryn had moved on again. But they had to at least try.

Being mid-afternoon, they would hopefully catch Jayden on his way home from school and avoid seeing Kathryn. *If they were still there.*

Ben sat quietly beside Tessa in the back seat of the taxi. Her palms were sweaty, as were his, despite the cool of the day.

"Nervous?" She looked up into his eyes.

He nodded, shifting in his seat.

She squeezed his hand.

She tried to steady her breathing as the taxi whizzed down the freeway and turned off into a suburb full of older apartments, many in need of a refurb. One corner block was covered in graffiti that someone had tried to remove without success, just making a bigger mess instead. Tessa jolted forward as a youth wearing torn jeans and a baseball cap backwards crossed the road ahead of them. He was listening to music by the way his head was moving. *Not Jayden, surely?* She turned her head as they passed and let out a breath. *Not Jayden.*

But surely they were in the wrong suburb? The Kathryn Ben had described wouldn't live in a suburb like this. *Would she?*

The taxi slowed, pulling up in front of an apartment building that looked the same as the others. Three stories high, dark brown brick. No garden. A row of mailboxes, some overflowing with junk mail possibly months old.

"Can you wait?" Ben leaned forward, offering the taxi driver money.

The taxi driver turned slightly in his seat and shook his head. "Got another job, sorry." He handed Ben a card. "Call when you're ready and I'll come back."

Ben paid the fare and thanked him before he sped off, leaving them standing on the pavement with their suitcase between them.

Tessa glanced at the building and her heart fell. Somehow she knew this was a mistake.

"What do we do?" She tried to keep her voice steady, but it wobbled a little.

"I'm not sure. Wait, I guess."

Tessa swallowed the lump in her throat. They stood out like sore thumbs. She shivered as a cold breeze hit them, picking up some of the loose junk mail, and sending it further down the street to lay there until another blast came through.

"Shall we knock?" Tessa lifted her gaze to Ben's. A look of hopelessness filled his eyes. She reached for his hand.

"A few minutes?"

She nodded. They shifted to the other side of the road and stood against a brick wall. A car rounded the corner and they both looked up. Kathryn? It kept driving. Tessa let out her breath.

A boy of about twelve on a skateboard stopped in front of them. "Can I help you?" His Texan drawl was heavily pronounced.

"Thanks, but we're waiting for someone." Ben's voice sounded so obviously Australian.

"Okay." The boy hopped back onto the board and skated off.

Minutes passed. The lump in Tessa's throat slipped to her stomach.

A long yellow bus came down the street and slowed, stopping a little to their right on the opposite side of the road. Tessa's pulse raced. They glanced at each other. *A school bus.*

The bus drove off. Three girls had hopped off and they chatted as they walked the other way. A boy of about Jayden's age stood checking his phone and then headed towards the apartment building.

Tessa's shoulders slumped. "It's not him."

"No."

"Maybe we could ask if he knows Jayden?" Tessa glanced at the boy disappearing up the stairs.

Ben's shoulders lifted. "It's worth a try." He picked up the suitcase and stepped off the curb.

Tessa took a breath and then sprinted across the road,

leaving Ben in her wake. "Excuse me. Hello." She held her hand against her chest and tried to catch her breath.

The boy stopped and turned around, his forehead puckering. "Me?"

"Yes, sorry. We," Tessa turned, motioning to Ben to hurry, "we were just wondering if you know a boy called Jayden? He's about your age, and he's Australian."

A shadow slipped across the boy's face. "Yeah, I knew him."

Ben placed the suitcase on the ground beside Tessa and stepped closer to the boy. "Knew him?"

The boy leaned on the railing, chewing gum. "Yeah. He lived here for a while, but then one day, he and his mom disappeared. Gone, just like that." He cocked his head. "You his dad?"

Tessa grabbed Ben's hand. The colour had drained from his face.

"Yes." Ben's voice was not much more than a whisper.

Tessa's heart thumped. This was their worst nightmare. She sucked in a breath and looked at the boy. "Do you know where they went?"

The boy shook his head and shrugged. "No idea. Like I said, they just disappeared. One day they were here, next day they were gone."

"Was Jayden..." Tessa gulped and took another breath. Her voice softened. "How was Jayden? Was he okay?"

"Yeah, he's a cool dude. Straight. A bit boring." He glanced at Ben. "Sorry."

The boy's comment brought a smile to Tessa's mouth and heartened her. She squeezed Ben's hand. Jayden was okay. They may not know where he was, but he was okay.

"Can you tell us anything else?"

The boy lifted his shoulder in a half shrug. "He talked about you sometimes. Said he missed you."

Tears pricked her eyes. She glanced at Ben. His Adam's apple bobbed in his throat.

"Anyway, I got to mind my little sister."

Tessa smiled warmly at the boy. "Thank you, ah… sorry, we didn't even get your name."

"Roger."

"Thank you, Roger. It's been great talking with you." Tessa twisted, pulling a notebook and a pen from her purse. "If you hear from him, could you let us know? I'll give you our contact details."

"Sure, but I doubt I will. They left before Christmas, and I haven't talked with him since."

"You never know. He might call."

Roger shrugged, but took the paper anyway.

"Thank you." She let out a deep sigh as Roger turned and headed on his way, lifting his hand in a half wave.

With Roger gone, Tessa turned and faced Ben. He looked crestfallen. His shoulders hung low and his eyes had a vacant stare. She stepped forward and wrapped her arms around, pulling him close. "At least we know he's okay."

Ben's chest rose and fell with measured breaths. Eventually he pulled away, staring at his hands momentarily before lifting his gaze to meet Tessa's.

"I want to lodge a missing person's file, Tess." He held her gaze. Despite the obvious heaviness of disappointment, his eyes held resolve.

She rubbed his arms. "That's a great idea." She didn't have the heart to say she thought it would be a waste of time.

. . .

BEN CALLED the number on the card given to him by the taxi driver, and within fifteen minutes they'd arrived at the local Police Station. It took an hour for the report to be lodged. With very few details available, they were given little chance of having Jayden and Kathryn found, but the police would put the alert out. They were officially listed as missing persons.

"I'd like to look for them," Ben said later that night after they'd settled into their hotel.

"And where would we start looking?" She held his gaze.

He exhaled slowly. "I have no idea."

"God knows where Jayden is. And he's okay. I feel it in my heart." Tears rolled from her eyes as the assurance that Jayden was truly okay settled deep within her.

# CHAPTER 21

*T*he next day, Ben and Tessa sat in the boarding lounge of Austin International Airport, waiting for their return flight to Guayaquil. Ben rubbed his forehead and drew a slow breath. "I feel like we failed him. If we'd gone earlier, we might have convinced him to come home."

"Oh Ben, don't start beating yourself up again. You know as well as I that we can't change the past." She squeezed his hand and gazed into his eyes. "But I have a sense of peace. I really believe Jayden's okay, wherever he is.

"You're always so confident, but I have my doubts." Ben drew another breath, letting it out slowly before lifting his chin. "But I'm determined not to let it get me down this time. I've learned a lot by being at the mission, and I know that all I can do now is leave Jayden in God's hands."

Tessa gave him the warmest smile, her eyes sparkling like they had when they first met at puppy classes which now seemed so long ago. Too much had happened since then.

"Ben," Tessa shifted in her seat, her expression growing serious. "I think I'd like to extend our time at the mission if we can. I don't know about you, but I'm not ready to go home yet."

He held her gaze, his mind ticking. The thought of going home to Brisbane without Jayden left a heaviness in his heart. Maybe Tess was right. Maybe they should stay longer. Images of the happy, smiling faces of the village children floated through his mind, bringing a smile to his lips. The children had brought such joy into both their lives, and the prospect of going home to a sterile, empty, quiet house held no appeal. His pulse quickened. Was this God's providence and leading? He'd never been one to actually feel God in his life; he was too practical for that, but being in the village where God was so real had helped him to open his heart to the spirit of God, changing him slowly from a facts and figures man to one who could feel. One who had compassion. And joy. And peace. Yes, despite some lingering doubts about whether Jayden would ever come home, peace was growing in his heart.

He took Tessa's hand and squeezed it. "I'm not either. I'd like to stay."

Tessa's eyes lit up. "Oh Ben, that's wonderful. I'm so happy!" Tears streamed down her cheeks as she threw her arms around him and hugged him.

BACK AT THE MISSION, Ben knocked tentatively on the office door.

Elliott and Larry had their heads down, deep in conversation.

"We'd better come back later," Ben whispered to Tessa.

Elliott looked up, his mouth curving into a smile as he caught sight of them. "Come in, come in."

"We don't want to intrude. We can come back later." Ben turned to leave.

"No, it's fine. Come in." Larry stood, motioning for them to take a seat.

"Thank you, Larry, Elliott." Ben shook their hands and took a seat. Tessa sat beside him. Since their discussion earlier that day, she hadn't been able to sit still, but he'd convinced her to let him take the lead.

"Sorry to hear about your son, Ben. It must have been heart-breaking for you." Larry's eyes were soft and his tone quiet.

Ben gulped. So much for his resolve to be strong. He cleared his throat. Tessa squeezed his hand. He drew a breath and let it out slowly. "Thank you, Larry. Yes, it was very disappointing, but we just have to trust he's okay and that he's eventually found." Ben swallowed the lump in his throat.

"We're all praying for you." Larry gave them both a genuinely warm smile.

"Thank you, we appreciate it."

"So, only a week left for you guys. We'll miss you." Larry straightened, crossing his legs.

Ben glanced quickly at Tessa. She gave him a nod as their eyes met. He turned his attention back to Larry and cleared his throat. "That's what we've come to talk about."

Elliott leaned forward, his eyes widening. "Have you decided to stay?"

Ben couldn't help himself—Elliott was so like Tess. He let out a chuckle. "How did you know?"

Elliott shrugged. "It gets in your blood. Once you get to know the people, it's hard to leave." His expression grew serious. "Plus I know how hard it must be for you to think about going home still not knowing anything about Jayden."

Ben drew a breath. "Yes, but we don't want to use the mission as an escape. We need to be useful. If you don't need us, we'll go home." He paused and glanced at Tessa. Her eyes were bright, filled with emotion. "We don't want to be a burden."

"You'd never be a burden. Either of you," Larry said quietly.

"Thank you, Larry. That's so kind." Tessa sniffed.

"Penny would love you to stay, Tessa. She's enjoyed having you here." Larry gave her a warm smile and turned his gaze to Ben. "And Ben, we've appreciated you, too. As far as I'm concerned, you can stay as long as you like. You're part of the family."

Ben's eyes flickered as a sense of belonging flowed through his body. It was nice to be appreciated and wanted, but what role would he play now that the playground and school were finished? Tessa had so many more skills than he. Maybe he could offer to do the mission's books. He returned Larry's smile. "Thank you, Larry. But what would you need us to do now that the playground's finished? I'm not sure I'm the best person for any more construction work." He let out a small chuckle as a memory of his first few days on the job flashed through his mind. They must have wondered why he'd volunteered.

"Oh, you did all right, Ben." Tessa slapped him fondly on the arm.

"Not so sure about that." He let out another chuckle before turning his attention back to Larry. "Any thoughts?"

"Well, the school needs English teachers. Most of the parents want their children to learn English as well as Spanish. The children already love you, and you're both highly educated, so I think you'd make a great fit."

"But we hardly know any Spanish!" Tessa straightened, her voice elevated.

"Time you started learning, sis." Elliott raised his brow, as if throwing out a challenge.

Larry leaned forward. "Sometimes it's good not to know too much. Children often learn quicker if they don't have a choice and they're forced to talk in English."

Tessa cocked her head, tucking a lock of hair behind her ear. "Guess that makes sense."

"And you could also take one of the mid-week Bible studies," Elliott said.

"As long as we don't need to take it in Spanish." Tessa chuckled. "What do you think, Ben?"

Ben cleared his throat. He'd never led a study group. Maybe he should have, but for whatever reason, he hadn't. Would he be up to it? Was his faith strong and genuine enough to be able to lead a study in God's word, and to encourage the people in their walk? He drew a slow breath, but his heart quickened. He'd be stretched, that was for sure. Definitely out of his comfort zone. *Why did I think they might want me to do the missions accounts?* Tessa squeezed his hand, her gaze fixed on him. She was waiting for an answer. He swallowed hard. *Okay God, if that's what you want me to do, I guess I'll do it.* "I think it's a great idea."

Tessa's face expanded into a beaming smile. If they'd been alone, Ben was sure she would have thrown her arms around him and kissed him.

"That's sorted then," Elliott said. "The new classrooms and playgrounds officially open next week, so it's a great time for you both to start."

BEN AND TESSA settled back into village life, thankful for the friendship and support of the team and the villagers. Jayden was never far from their thoughts, and they prayed for him continually, but their hearts were full of God's love and peace, confident that he was not only caring for them, but for Jayden too, wherever he was.

On Monday morning, they were on hand to welcome the children attending their first day of formal learning. Mayta, Santiago, Juan, and the others whispered and giggled as they filed into the school in freshly cleaned clothes.

Maria took the morning classes of basic Math, Science, Social Studies and History subjects. The children were eager to learn and quick to memorize any number of facts or figures placed before them. After lunch, Ben and Tessa commenced the English lessons. Tessa quickly grew to love the time they spent teaching the children, and looked forward to being with them every weekday. She enjoyed being around their happy, innocent spirits, and cheered just as loud as they did when they learned how to correctly pronounce a new word or write their names without any help from her or Ben.

They also readily stepped into their roles as midweek Bible

study leaders. After the first few times, Ben's concern soon subsided. "I don't see why I was so nervous, really," he told her one afternoon as they cleaned up the school building at the end of a long day of teaching. "The people here have such genuine faith, and they aren't expecting perfection from me," he continued. "They're happy to simply study the Word and learn more about God. I've learned more from them than the other way around."

"You aren't the only one." Tessa rubbed the last bit of chalk off the board and then turned around, blowing hair off her forehead. "I'm glad we stayed. I really am."

Ben stepped towards her, a glint in his eye. "You look very appealing with chalk all over your face, Mrs. Williams." He lifted his hand and brushed her face with the tips of his fingers.

Tessa's body tingled. "Ben! Remember where we are!"

He glanced around and stepped closer. "I don't see any kids, do you?" He cupped her face gently in his hands and lowered his mouth against hers.

Happy sounds of children's laughter from the playground outside filled her ears, but love for Ben filled her heart as he kissed her tenderly.

# CHAPTER 22

*J*ayden's school was in town, and at first, Kathryn dropped him off on her way to work. He mostly kept to himself, not bothering to join any sports teams or extra school activities. After school, he avoided going home until he absolutely had to, hanging out at the mall or the park, and then, if Mum didn't pick him up, he'd trudge the two miles home. When Buck stayed over, which he often did, Jayden took to eating his meals in his room.

Angry, slurred words often came from the living room. One night, Buck was particularly obnoxious. "Where's the kid. Katy?

Jayden jumped out of bed, made sure his door was locked, and pushed his small nightstand in front of it. His heart pounded as Buck fumbled with the doorknob, and then started banging on it. "Open the door, kid. Let me in."

"Buck, leave Jay alone." Mum's voice sounded so pitiful against Buck's. "He's sleeping. Don't bother him."

"Shut up, woman. I don't need you telling me what to do."

Mum said something back to Buck, but Jayden couldn't hear her words. He covered his head with his pillow to block out the rest of their arguing as they moved away from his door. Several loud crashes made him jump. His heart raced. It sounded like they were throwing things at each another. They got louder.

"Stop it, or I'll call the police." Mum sounded scared.

Buck laughed and swore. "And then what'll you do, Kate? I own this house, don't forget."

Jayden huddled under his blankets, praying they'd stop.

He must have drifted off to sleep, but the sound of the front door slamming woke him. A car started in the driveway and sped off, sending gravel flying as the wheels spun out. Had Buck left, or was it Mum? He hoped it was Buck. He didn't want to be left alone in the house with that creature.

Jayden slid out of bed and carefully pushed back the table from in front of his bedroom door and unlocked it. He peeked out and listened before stepping fully into the hall. "Mum." His voice was little more than a whisper. No answer.

He checked her bedroom. The bed was a mess and the air reeked of cigarette smoke, but it was empty. He crept along the hall towards the kitchen. He gasped. Both the kitchen and living room were a disaster. Chairs and dishes had been thrown every which way and broken glass lay strewn all over the floor.

"Mum." Jayden called louder this time. Seemed Buck wasn't there, but Mum didn't appear to be either. His mind raced. Where was she? What if Buck had done something terrible to her? He carefully stepped over some glass and checked the bathroom. Empty. Nowhere else to check but the barn. He retraced his steps and looked inside her bedroom again.

A faint whimper sounded from the direction of the closet.

"Mum, is that you?" He switched on the light. The closet door was slightly ajar. He flung it open. He gasped. Crouched in a corner, sobbing, Mum looked up, her face swollen and bruised.

"Is he gone?" She gulped back sobs.

"Yes." Jayden helped her to her feet.

She wobbled before sinking onto the bed and wrapping her arms around her middle.

"How could you let him do this to you?" Jayden sat beside her, placing his arm around her shoulder.

Mum shrugged. "He'll be okay when he sobers up." She closed her eyes and breathed slowly. "I'll be fine."

"We need to get out of this town. I told you he was nothing but trouble." Jayden sucked in a breath. "You need to get rid of him, Mum. If you don't, I'll be leaving."

"Jay, please don't." She wrapped her arms around him and clung to him. "We can all live together just fine."

"No, we can't." Jayden pushed back angry tears. Why couldn't she see that Buck was no good for her? "Look at yourself. Look what he's done to you. You need to get rid of him."

Mum lifted a hand and touched the bruise on her swollen lip. She shook her head. "I can't do that, Jay. I wouldn't survive without him."

Jayden let out a frustrated sigh. This was it, then. "Fine, if you won't make Buck leave, I'm going." He left her room and went back into his bedroom. He pulled out his old lime-green and black duffle bag and began stuffing his clothes and other belongings into it.

"Don't leave, Jay, please." She collapsed in the doorway and sobbed.

Jayden sighed, his resolve weakening. Mum needed him. What would that creep do to her if he wasn't there to look out for her?

"Fine, I'll stay until I get a job and we can afford a place of our own." He glared at her. "But you need to find another job, too."

"Thank you. Jay. I will." Tears streamed down her cheeks. Jayden felt like vomiting.

JAYDEN SPENT ALL his free time scouring the newspapers for jobs. A number of stores and restaurants had 'Now Hiring' signs in their windows; the one at Value Village said they needed stockers, so he applied for that one.

For the next few days, he continued going to school while he waited to hear about the job. As expected, Mum hadn't looked for anything else.

One day his phone rang. It was the Value Village thrift store manager. He'd got the job.

# CHAPTER 23

*I*'ve got a job, Mum, and I'll be leaving as soon as I can afford a place of my own." Jayden waited for her reaction as he buttered some toast that evening. Buck wasn't there, and for once Mum was sober.

Mum drew her eyebrows together. "Jay... you can't do that."

"I am, and you can't stop me. I'll have enough money within a week or so. I'd like you to come with me, but that's up to you.

A shadow crossed her face. "I can't, Jay." Her voice was quiet, timid.

He stopped buttering and crossed his arms. "Buck is no good for you. When are you going to see that?"

"He loves me, Jay."

Jayden sighed heavily. "Yeah right. That's why you're covered in bruises."

She rubbed her arms. "He doesn't mean it."

"Well, I'm leaving as soon as I can. You can choose what you do."

. . .

JAYDEN STARTED his job the next day. The manager welcomed him and introduced him to a middle-age woman with glossy black curls standing behind one of the registers. "Charmian will do your orientation and give you a tour. Welcome aboard." The manager shook his hand and left him with Charmian.

She gave him a tour of the store before signing him in and doing the paperwork. His hand shook as he handed her the fake ID Mum had given him a while back. Charmian didn't blink and handed him a navy blue polo shirt with his nametag on it. "We're also in need of baggers in the afternoons, so if you want to work double time you can. Don't worry, you'll be paid for it."

"I'd be glad to do double-work. I really need the money. I'm trying to pay for my own apartment."

Charmian's eyebrows came together as she studied him. "You're a bit young to be living on your own."

"It's complicated." Jayden shrugged. Should he confide in her? It'd been so long since he'd had someone he could talk to, and Charmian seemed nice enough. Maybe he could tell her just a little. "I can't live with my mum anymore, so I'm trying to find a place of my own."

"I see." Charmian drew a breath. "Where are you staying now?"

Jayden gulped as the to-do he'd had with Mum that morning flashed through his mind. He'd tried once more to make her see how bad Buck was, and had tried to convince her again to be rid of him, but she'd refused, and he'd stormed out. He lowered his gaze and fidgeted with his hands. "I don't

exactly have anywhere to stay at the moment. But I can probably stay with one of my classmates for a couple of days, just
until I get sorted."

Charmian eyed him up and down, her expression softening. "You're welcome to stay with me until you get on your
feet. I have three boys of my own and I'm sure they won't mind
sharing the house with you for a while."

Tears pricked his eyes. He pushed them back. "Thanks, but
I'll be fine."

"If you say so, but the offer stands." She gave him a warm
smile. "I know what it's like to be a teenager on your own. My
parents were druggies and I wouldn't have survived if some
kind people hadn't helped me out. It isn't easy trying to do life
on your own, so if you change your mind and need a place to
stay and something to eat, my home is open to you." She picked
up a notepad, tore a sheet out, and scribbled down her address.
"Here, keep this in case you need it."

"Thanks." Jayden swallowed the lump in his throat. He took
the paper and folded it into his pocket. "I'd better start work
now, if that's okay."

She smiled at him. "Of course."

Jayden walked to the first shelf that needed restocking. He
took a deep breath. Was God answering his prayers already?
The job, the offer of a place to stay until he could afford his
own. He shook his head. No, he wasn't prepared to believe that
God was behind it all, but he was thankful that there were
people in the world like Charmian who actually cared about
others. Not everyone was selfish and pathetic like Mum.

After working all day, he decided to accept Charmian's
offer. She gave him a spare bedroom and told him he could

stay there as long as he needed. Her three boys were much younger than him, but they, along with Charmian's husband, made him feel welcome.

He kept an eye on Mum from a distance and hoped that one day she'd see sense. He still felt a responsibility for her, even though she didn't deserve it. Why she chose to stay with Buck was beyond him. But he couldn't leave her altogether. She was his mother, after all.

Although he enjoyed his time at Charmian's, Jayden was eager to move into his own place. After working hard for two months, he had enough money to pay for his own small apartment.

"I WISH you'd continue with your education," Charmian said as Jayden ate breakfast at her house for the last time. He'd already packed his belongings and was ready to move into his own place. "You can at least go to school in the mornings and then work in the afternoons."

He shrugged. "It doesn't matter. I'll be fine. One day I'll go to college and study for a proper job. I'd like to be a vet one day."

"That's a worthy thing to aim for." She gave him a warm smile. "Make sure you do that. Don't give up on your dreams."

He nodded. She was right. He shouldn't give up on his dreams, but right now he just needed to survive.

"You'll still come by and play with us sometimes, won't you?" the oldest of Charmian's three sons asked.

"I'll try to."

Her younger two sons gave him a hug before he left. "Bye,

Jayden, we'll miss you."

He laughed as he returned their hugs. "I'll miss you guys, too."

Even though he'd bought a three-speed bike with part of the money he'd earned, Charmian insisted on driving him to his apartment. "A bicycle doesn't have a trunk. Where will you put your bags if we don't take my car?"

"Okay, you win."

"I really appreciate your help," Jayden said when they pulled up in front of the apartment complex and he climbed out of her car.

"I'm glad I could be of some help on your journey." She smiled at him, her eyes glistening. "Take care of yourself now. I'll see you Monday at the store."

Jayden waved goodbye. He checked to make sure that his bicycle was securely locked to the grid bike rack and then went up the stairs, found his apartment number, and unlocked the door. It was only a one-bedroom apartment, and compared to all the places he'd lived in before, it was tiny, but it was his. He didn't have to worry about living with people he didn't want to live with. Especially people called Buck.

He worked six days a week and soon became familiar with many of the customers who frequented the store. In turn, they became used to seeing him there and often asked him for help finding certain items or taking things out to their cars. In particular, a pretty red-haired girl who seemed to be about his age, maybe a little older, caught his attention. He finally worked up the courage and made an attempt to get to know her. "Hey, I've seen you here a lot," he said one evening while bagging her purchases. "Do you live around here?"

"About ten miles out of town." Her eyes were on him as he placed the groceries into the bag.

His hands shook as he placed a tub of sugar into the bag.

"What about you? Where do you live?" Her voice was soft like silk.

"Just a few blocks away." He lifted his head. "My name's Jayden, by the way."

The girl raised an eyebrow. "I know that. It's on your nametag." Her eyes twinkled.

"Oh, right." He let out a nervous chuckle. "Well, what's your name?"

"Angela. Angela Morgan. "I know you said you live around here, but you're not from here."

"No, I'm Australian."

"Thought so. What are you doing all the way up here?"

Jayden scratched his head and smiled. He should have known this was coming. "It's a long story."

"I like long stories. Maybe we can get together sometime and you can tell me. I found this new ice-cream place I'm dying to try. Maybe we can meet there, say on Saturday, and you can tell me your story then?"

"I'd like that, but I have to work on Saturday."

She shrugged. "We can go on Sunday. I'm sure you don't have to work then."

"Sunday afternoon would be great." Jayden had finished bagging her purchases and she was ready to go. "Would you like me to take these out for you?" She nodded, a warm smile sitting on her pretty face. He walked outside with her, pushing the cart in front of him. She indicated the red car sitting in the middle of the car park. "It's actually my mom's car, but I'm learning to drive. She'll be back in a few minutes."

Jayden loaded the bags into the back seat of the car. As he lifted his head, he noticed a cross hanging from the interior rearview mirror. He gulped. Why did she have to come from a religious family?

He straightened and nodded to it. "Are you Christian?"

Angela's eyes lit up. "Yes! Are you?"

Jayden took a slow breath. If he was truthful, he'd have to answer 'no'. But something had definitely been moving inside him of late, and he'd been wondering if it was God. She was waiting for an answer. He had to say something. "Kind of."

Angela gave him a quizzical look. "What do you mean, *kind of?* You can't be a 'kind of' Christian."

"Dunno." Jayden shrugged. "Maybe we can talk about it sometime."

"I'd love to." Her face lit up as she gave him another smile. "See you Sunday, oh, and thanks for your help."

"My pleasure." Jayden's heart raced as he walked back to the store. He couldn't believe it—he had a date with a pretty girl called Angela. He couldn't wipe the smile off his face.

THE REST of the week passed ever so slowly. Sunday seemed to be so far away, but finally it came. Jayden finished work at one o'clock, and quickly rode back to his apartment and showered. He slipped on the new pair of jeans and a white t-shirt he'd bought for the occasion. Kind of boring, but Dad always looked smart dressed like that, and besides, he felt comfortable in them. He stood in front of the mirror and combed his hair, now much shorter because of the job. He looked pretty good for his first date. What would Dad and Tessa think if they could see him now? No time for regrets, Angela would be waiting for him.

The ice-cream shop was within walking distance, so he chose to walk instead of riding. It was a quaint blue building that sold handmade ice cream in a variety of flavors. Angela was already there, sitting outside at a table underneath an umbrella. She lifted her hand and waved. All of a sudden, his heart thumped and his hands grew clammy. He took a deep breath and joined her at the table. Angela had clear green eyes that seemed to sparkle all the time. Her red hair was loose and bounced on her shoulders. She was beautiful, but he got the feeling that unlike Britney, she wasn't even aware of it.

"Sorry I'm late." He knew he sounded nervous.

Angela tilted her head. "You're not late. I was early. Mom and Dad dropped me in town after lunch."

"Oh."

"I'm going to have Caramel Honeycomb. What would you like?"

Jayden quickly glanced at the board. "I'll have Berry. But let me get them." He rose and joined the line. His heart still hadn't stopped thumping. He placed the order and then carried them back to the table.

"So, tell me the story of why you're here." Angela looked at him over her cone, her alluring green eyes fixed on.

Jayden took a breath and began the story of how he'd ended up in Hunters Hollow. Angela's forehead wrinkled as he told her about his mother and Buck, and a concerned expression grew on her face.

"Do you miss your Dad and stepmom? I know I would." She looked down at her hands and inspected her fingernails before lifting her gaze to his. "I don't like everything about my parents, but I don't think I could leave them and not have any contact with them. That would be pretty hard."

Jayden grimaced. Telling Angela the whole story had stirred feelings inside him; he didn't know if he could talk anymore without breaking down. And he didn't want to do that in front of her, especially on their first date. Truth was, he'd been thinking more about calling Dad of late, since he'd moved away from Mum and Buck. He did miss both him and Tessa, but did he want to admit that to Angela? Not yet. He drew a steadying breath, releasing it slowly. "I would like to see them again, I just don't know when."

Angela gave him a smile that told him she understood. "I told my parents about you, Jayden. They said they'd like to meet you. Would you like to come to dinner sometime this week?"

His eyes widened. Was she just taking pity on him? He held her gaze. No, he didn't think so. *But was he ready to meet her parents?* He was about to say no, but then changed his mind. He liked her. There was something genuine about her, and he got the feeling her folks would be the same, as long as they didn't judge him or try preaching at him. "Yeah, sure, that would be great. Thank you."

She smiled at him again. "How about Wednesday?"

"Works for me."

"We'll pick you up."

"Thanks, but I can ride."

She chuckled. "Suit yourself, it's a long way."

He straightened. "I'm trying to get fit." And now he really had a reason to.

ANY CONCERNS that Jayden had of being judged by Angela's parents quickly dissipated the instant he stepped into their house. They welcomed him warmly, and before long, he found himself opening up to them. They reminded him of Telford and Eleanor, even though they were a few years younger than Tessa's parents, and he felt he could trust their hospitable and sincere personalities. After Mrs. Morgan's roast dinner had been served, he told them the same story he'd told Angela, but this time included how he felt about it all. It was a relief to finally be able to talk with someone about the choices he'd made, and he was glad to at last share his feelings with people who truly wanted to listen and understand.

"I really miss my dad and Tessa a lot, but it was my decision to leave." He paused, taking a breath. "Sometimes I wish I'd never gone, but I can't go back and change the past. But now I feel responsible for my mum, like I need to keep an eye on her, or at least be close by if she needs me. Besides, it'd be difficult to go home and face my dad and Tessa now."

"It's always difficult to say sorry," Mrs. Morgan said as she put her knife and fork down. "But we always feel better once we do."

Jayden remained silent, his mind spinning. Was he just making excuses for not going back?

Mr. Morgan leaned forward. "It's true you can't go back and have a new beginning, but you can start now and have a good ending." He paused, holding Jayden's gaze. "Why don't you start by writing them a letter?"

A sense of relief flowed through Jayden. He'd thought Mr. Morgan was going to start preaching at him. But a letter? Yes, he could do that.

On his ride home later that night, Jayden stopped at about the halfway mark and climbed off his bike. The moon was already high in the sky, just a half-moon, but still enough to shed light on the valley. Somewhere over there, up one of the smaller, hidden valleys, sat the cottage where Mum and Buck still lived. He'd seen her several times on the street, and each time he couldn't believe she was the same person who'd whisked him away in that fancy private jet less than a year ago. She no longer looked like a model; her designer wardrobe had been replaced with charity store clothes, and her once shining blonde hair was now dull and tinged with grey. But he still couldn't leave her. Not yet.

He gazed up at the stars, and began to wonder what life was all about. Could he believe in the God he'd learned about in Sunday School, the God he'd been told had created all of this? The God that Dad and Tessa believed in, that Angela and her parents believed in, or was there no God and it had just all happened like he'd been taught in school? Did God really exist, or was he just a crutch? Jayden couldn't deny the feeling he'd had in that church that God was speaking to him, but maybe it had just been his imagination, his need at the time. He let out a huge sigh. Too much to think about tonight. He needed to go home and start that letter. He stood up and climbed back onto his bike and rode the remainder of the distance, composing it in his mind. *Dear Dad and Tessa...*

# CHAPTER 24

*W*hen Tessa began struggling with all day sickness a few weeks later, she scarcely dared let herself believe she could be pregnant again, but the signs were obvious. She tried to hide it the best she could, but waves of nausea swept over her as she taught the children in the afternoons, a feeling made worse by the persistent humidity. When accompanying Penny on one of her medical rounds, she had to excuse herself and hurry outside to find a private place to vomit.

"Tess, are you okay?" Ben asked one evening during dinner. For the second day in a row, she was toying with her food and only managed a few spoonful. "You're not ill, are you?"

"No, I just haven't been very hungry lately. I think it may be the heat." She hadn't wanted to get his hopes up, perhaps only to find out later it wasn't true after-all. But maybe she should tell him. She was almost one hundred percent sure.

He tilted his head, narrowing his eyes. "Really?"

She pushed her hair off her face and lifted her gaze. Her heart raced. She needed to tell him. She took his hand and looked into his eyes, a coy grin growing on her face. "Ben," she paused, "I think I'm pregnant."

His eyes lit up. He jumped up and threw his arms around her, hugging her tightly, laughing and crying at once.

"I only think," she said in a happy whisper. "I'm not completely sure."

"This is wonderful news. The best. We have to let everyone know."

"Not yet!" She leaned out of his embrace, gently touching his lips with her fingers. "Not until we know for sure and I'm past the danger period."

Ben's expression sobered. "You're right. I'm sorry. I just wanted to shout the news to everyone."

"I know, but it's too early yet, and besides, I haven't even been to the doctor."

"Okay. Our secret for now. But we need to get you to the doctor." He pulled her head forward and gently kissed the top of her head.

"Thanks."

ELLIOTT DROVE them to Guayaquil the next day. It just so happened he had to go to the city for a meeting, so it fitted in perfectly. They told him it was just for 'women's business'. The glint in his eye suggested he'd guessed, but for once he didn't press them. Penny stepped in and took their English class.

"Well, you're just over seven weeks and everything looks fine," the doctor said as he ran the ultrasound monitor over

Tessa's stomach. She held back tears as she studied the grainy black and grey image of the tiny fetus growing inside her. Seeing the heartbeat gave her hope that this time she could carry it to full term.

"Do you suggest we leave Ecuador and return home to Australia?" Ben asked.

The doctor glanced up. "I don't see a need at the moment, unless of course you'd like to. I can't foresee any complications, and as long as you take care of yourself, Miss Tessa, you should be fine."

Tessa smiled and nodded. Of course she'd take care of herself!

"Perhaps you should return to Australia about three to four months before the baby's due, assuming you want to be home for the birth."

She caught Ben's eye. Yes, that would be perfect.

Sitting in between Elliott and Ben on the return ride from the hospital back to the mission grounds, Tessa's heart was full. She linked her arm with Ben's, and ran her other hand over her belly that was still flat but held a special little person. *Their baby.*

TESSA WAS ON CLOUD NINE, although she had to force herself not to think about the possibility of miscarrying again. The doctor had assured her she was in perfect health, and there was no reason to worry. But that's what the doctor had said the last time.

It was hard to hide the pregnancy from Penny. She was a nurse, after all.

"You're very lucky," Penny said to her one day in between visits as they sat under some shady palm trees beside the river.

"What do you mean?" Tessa looked at her, trying to act innocent.

"I know you're expecting." Penny's eyes twinkled. "Congratulations, sweet girl. I'm so happy for you." She reached out and squeezed Tessa's hand.

Tessa gave her a grateful smile. "Thank you. We were going to start telling people soon now I'm almost past the danger period." Tessa felt her lip quiver.

Penny narrowed her eyes. "Are you worried?"

Tessa sucked in a breath. Did it show that much? Her shoulders slumped. "Just a little. I miscarried last year, so it's on my mind a lot, although I'm trying to stay positive."

"Oh Tessa, I'm so sorry. But there's no reason for it to happen again, is there?"

"No, the doctor said everything's fine. I'm just being silly." Tessa blinked back tears. She had no rational reason to be concerned, but the memory of that night was still so vivid sometimes, and even though she knew their little baby boy was in heaven, waiting for her and Ben, the pain of loss was still so real.

"Come here. Let me give you a hug." Penny drew her into her arms, but as she did, tears streamed down Tessa's cheeks. She couldn't help it. Penny reminded her so much of her mother. And that's what she needed. Her mother's arms.

"There, there, you'll be fine." Penny whispered into her ear.

Tessa sniffed as she nodded. She wiped her eyes with a tissue she pulled from her pocket.

"You know, Larry and I were unable to have children." Penny's voice was soft and quiet.

Tessa straightened, wiping her eye again. "I'm so sorry. I had no idea." She'd assumed they'd chosen not to have children. She felt so bad.

"There was no reason for you to know. We'd so much wanted a large family, but it wasn't to be." Penny smiled wistfully. "We've come to accept it now, but in the early days it was hard. Both Larry and I questioned God continually. We couldn't understand why he wouldn't bless us with a baby. We tried everything, but in the end, we just had to come to terms with it and accept that it was God's will for our lives. And you know, God has blessed our lives so much, but in a completely different way to what we'd ever imagined."

Tessa took a deep breath as she allowed Penny's words to sink in. Everyone had challenges, some more obvious than others, but they were all part of the journey called life. She recalled the hymn she'd sung with Stephanie, and the words challenged her yet again. Would her anchor hold, even if she did miscarry again? What if it had turned out that she and Ben couldn't have children, like Penny and Larry? And what if Jayden never returned? Not that she believed he wouldn't. But would her anchor hold, regardless? Could she go back home and live confidently with Jesus as her Lord and Saviour, trusting him like the people of this village did on a daily basis for the simplest of things that she and Ben had taken for granted all their lives? She wanted to. She truly did.

The pain of the loss of their first baby was still a dull ache in her chest. She guessed it would always be, but now they had another precious little one growing inside her. She had nothing to be sad or concerned about. She and Ben had their whole futures ahead of them. Instead of being bitter about not having children, Penny's disappointment had made her stronger, with a heart to serve and love God and to serve and love others. Wasn't that the reason she and Ben had come to Ecuador? To get their minds off their own problems and to serve others? *God, please forgive me for my lack of trust. Give me a heart for others, just like Penny, and make me a better, stronger person, so I can serve you and others with compassion and fervour. You are my anchor, Lord God, steadfast and sure. I will hold firmly to You, and trust You, regardless of what happens in my life.*

"Thank you, Penny." Tessa sniffed again. "That spoke to me so much. You're such a wonderful person. Thank you for being here for me."

"Oh Tessa, you'll make me cry next. Come on, let's get going. Our rounds won't do themselves, you know."

Penny stood and held her hand out to Tessa before giving her another hug. "We'll be praying for you, Tessa."

Tessa blew her nose and smiled. "Thank you so much."

THAT NIGHT, Tessa rested her head against Ben's chest as he read. Outside, the noises of the night drifted in. Somewhere in the distance, a cow bellowed. Someone played a drum not far away, and next door, a baby cried. She'd miss the closeness of community living, but it was time. She lifted her head and turned Ben's face toward her. "Ben..."

"I'm trying to read." He turned his face back to his book.

"I want to say something."

"What?" He kept reading.

"I'm ready to go home."

He jolted up, dropping his book and losing his place. "Really?"

Tessa nodded, her eyes misting over.

Ben's eyes softened. "I've been thinking the same thing. It's time, isn't it?" He lifted his hand and ran his fingers slowly down her hairline as he held her gaze.

She nodded again, happy tears filling her eyes. Lowering her head back onto Ben's chest, she sighed contentedly as he wrapped his arms around her.

# CHAPTER 25

*B*en and Tessa broke the news to the team the following day. Nobody wanted them to go, but everyone respected their decision, especially when they heard about the new addition. The soon-to-be-parents agreed to stay until new team members had been recruited.

The evening before their departure, the mission put on a huge going away party. Early in the morning, fires were lit, and four pigs prepared. The women busied themselves cooking an array of dishes to accompany the roast pig, and also prepared platters of the fresh tropical fruit that Tessa had come to love. She'd miss the gaiety and colour of village life, but mostly she'd miss the people. They'd made so many wonderful friends, but her focus was now turning to their baby and life back home.

The party carried on well into the night, with lots of eating, music and dancing. One by one, the children and their parents offered their shy goodbyes, presenting small handmade gifts to remember them by. Tessa was nearly brought to tears several times, but when Maria gave her a handwritten recipe book, she couldn't hold them back any longer. "Maria, you have been such a special friend. Thank you." She wiped her tears with a tissue and then gave Maria a big hug.

"We'll miss you, Tessa. We all will. Come back sometime soon?"

Tessa nodded. Yes, she'd like that.

Larry called everyone to attention after dessert had been served, motioning for her and Ben to join him.

Tessa grabbed Ben's hand as they stepped towards Larry. Her heart was heavy as reality hit her. They were actually leaving this place they'd come to love so much. Tomorrow they'd be back in their clean, quiet house in suburban Brisbane, far away from this colourful, noisy village. But it was time. She knew that. And as Larry and Penny gave their farewell speeches and prayed for them, she knew in her heart that this was God's timing.

As ELLIOTT DROVE them to the airport the following morning, Tessa drank in the colours and sights and sounds of the countryside, entrusting them to her memory. She'd never forget this place nor its people. She squeezed Ben's hand. They'd hardly said a word. Even Elliott was unusually subdued.

"I'm going to miss you, sis." Elliott's eyes misted over as he gave her one last hug.

"We're going to miss you, too. Thank you for everything." She smiled into his eyes and sucked in a breath. "Come and visit soon? I know Mum would love to see you."

He nodded and waved as they turned and walked toward the Departures area.

CIRCLING above Brisbane just over twenty-four hours later, Tessa gazed down on her hometown with excitement, although a tinge of sadness sat in her heart. The most difficult part of the trip had been the transit in Los Angeles. Both she and Ben couldn't help but wonder if Jayden was nearby, but they had no way of knowing. He'd had no communication with Neil or anyone else for months, and so they had no choice but to continue trusting that he was okay.

Eleanor and Telford met them at the airport, and Tessa once again couldn't control her emotions and teared up at first sight of her parents. Her mother gave her a big hug and congratulated her on her pregnancy. Her father wrapped her in a bear hug and told her how much he'd missed them both.

After catching up over a light lunch at Bussey's, her parents delivered them home, promising to come by again in the next day or so once they'd recovered from the flight.

Stepping inside their house, Tessa's eyes popped. It was huge. And so white. And so clean.

Ben slipped his arms around her and nuzzled her neck. "What say we brighten it up?"

Tessa nodded as she gazed around. "Yes, no more white!"

Ben laughed and turned her around. "Well, Mrs. Williams, this is another beginning."

She gazed into Ben's eyes and lifted her hand to his cheek. "I'm happy to be home, Ben."

"So am I."

Her body tingled as he leaned down and kissed her gently on the lips. She chuckled when he swept her off her feet and carried her upstairs to their bedroom. "You could never have done that before we went to Ecuador!"

He laughed as he lowered her onto their king-sized bed, but then his expression sobered as he gazed into her eyes. "I didn't think I could love you more than I did on our wedding day, but I do. I love you so much." He stroked her cheek gently with his fingers. Her heart thumped as he continued. "Thank you for supporting me when I was so miserable, and always believing in me. I wouldn't have survived without you." His eyes moistened, causing hers to do the same.

"Oh Ben. Stop your talking and just kiss me." She pulled his head down and buried herself in his love.


THE COUPLE who'd rented their home had kept the house and yard in good condition, and Jayden's bedroom was still untouched and remained just the way he'd left it, a condition of the rental agreement.

"So much mail." Tessa sighed as she began checking the pile she'd ignored over the few days since they'd returned. "I certainly didn't miss this while we were away."

"Me either." Ben pulled up a chair and started sorting through the pile. Tessa chuckled when he began placing the mail into neat stacks. Some things would never change.

"I'll get that," Tessa said as the phone rang. She swung into the hall and picked up the receiver. "Hi, Tess," Fran greeted from the other end. "I'm glad you're back. Did you enjoy your time away?" Fran's tone was still so business like, although there was a tinge of warmth to her voice.

"Very much so." Tessa smiled as a memory of the village flashed through her mind. "We actually really loved it." Her heart warmed as she gazed at the assorted handmade gifts now taking pride of place on the display cabinet in the living room.

"I'm glad you had a good time. Just a quick call to touch base and to run something past you."

"Yes..."

"We've been unusually busy, so I've hired two more employees." Fran paused and cleared her throat. "Harrison's been doing a fantastic job as manager. You chose the right person to take over while you were away. I was actually thinking I'd like to keep him on as manager, at least for a time."

Tessa pressed her lips together and tried to steady her breathing. *Is Fran actually saying what I think she's saying? She wants to replace me with Harrison as manager? Didn't she think I was the best person for the job?*

"However, Harrison can't manage effectively while also being head surgeon, so if you'd like to return to your old job, he could certainly use your help." Fran paused. "Any thoughts on that?"

Tessa pondered her response before replying. She had to admit she was put out, but hadn't she promised God to trust Him, regardless? Maybe this had been put before her to test her resolve. She could react badly, make a scene, or just accept the situation gracefully. She didn't have to be manager. She still had a job she loved, and she should be grateful. Besides, she'd be stopping work shortly anyway. Placing her hand on her tummy, she caressed the baby growing inside her. "I think that's a fine decision, Fran. Harrison has great skills, and I'll look forward to getting my gloves back on. Oh, and also, I'm pregnant."

Fran remained silent for a few seconds before congratulating her. "I guess it was the right decision then." She let out a small laugh.

"Tess, Tess! Come quickly!" Ben called from the kitchen.

"I've got to go, Fran. Talk soon." Tessa hung up and ran to the kitchen where Ben was holding up an envelope, his eyes brimming.

"It's from Jayden. He wrote us a letter."

Tessa's heart pounded as she took the envelope and inspected it. "It's dated two weeks ago. And he's way up north. How did he get there?"

"He explains it all in the letter. I've quickly scanned it. He's okay. He's found a job and is staying in his own place, but he's also looking after Kathryn. He says he can't leave her right now for some reason. I don't know why, but I have the feeling he's not happy with her anymore."

Tessa sat down and quickly read through Jayden's entire letter for herself, wiping tears from her eyes as she read. She lifted her eyes to Ben's and smiled though her tears. "I believe this means he'll be coming home sometime soon."

"I think you're right. I truly do."

**Ben, Tessa and Jayden's story continues in...**

**BOOK 4: "TRIUMPHANT LOVE"**

## *NOTE FROM THE AUTHOR*

Hi! It's Juliette here. I hope you've enjoyed the third book in "The True Love Series". Ben, Tessa and Jayden's stories continue in Book 4 - "Triumphant Love" (free to read on Kindle Unlimited).

Make sure you're on my readers' email list so you don't miss notifications of my new releases! If you haven't joined yet, you can do so at www.julietteduncan.com/subscribe and you'll also receive a free copy of *"HANK AND SARAH - A LOVE STORY"* as a thank you gift for joining.

**Enjoyed Tormented Love? You can make a big difference...**

Help other people find this book by writing a review and telling them why you liked it. Honest reviews of my books help bring them to the attention of other readers just like yourself, and I'd be very grateful if you could spare just five minutes to leave a review (it can be as short as you like).

BLESSINGS,

Juliette

# OTHER BOOKS BY JULIETTE DUNCAN

**Find all of Juliette Duncan's books on her website:**
www.julietteduncan.com/library

## True Love Series

*Tender Love*

*Tested Love*

*Tormented Love*

*Triumphant Love*

## Precious Love Series

*Forever Cherished*

*Forever Faithful*

*Forever His*

## Water's Edge Series

*When I Met You*

A barmaid searching for purpose, a youth pastor searching for love

*Because of You*

When dreams are shattered, can hope be re-found?

*With You Beside Me*

A doctor on a mission, a young woman wrestling with God, and an illness that touches the entire town.

*All I Want is You*

A young widow trusting God with her future.

A handsome property developer who could be the answer to her prayers…

*It Was Always You*

She was in love with her dead sister's boyfriend. He treats her like his kid sister.

*My Heart Belongs to You*

A jilted romance author and a free-spirited surfer, both searching for something more…

**A Sunburned Land Series**

A mature-age romance series

*Slow Road to Love*

A divorced reporter on a remote assignment. An alluring cattleman who captures her heart…

*Slow Path to Peace*

With their lives stripped bare, can Serena and David find peace?

*Slow Ride Home*

He's a cowboy who lives his life with abandon. She's spirited and fiercely independent…

*Slow Dance at Dusk*

A death, a wedding, and a change of plans…

*Slow Trek to Triumph*

A road trip, a new romance, and a new start…

*Christmas at Goddard Downs*

A Christmas celebration, an engagement in doubt…

**The Shadows Series**

A jilted teacher, a charming Irishman, & the chance to escape their pasts & start again.

*Lingering Shadows*

*Facing the Shadows*

*Beyond the Shadows*

*Secrets and Sacrifice*

*A Highland Christmas*

### A Time For Everything Series

A mature-age Christian Romance series

*A Time to Treasure*

She lost her husband and misses him dearly. He lost his wife but is ready to move on. Will a chance meeting in a foreign city change their lives forever?

*A Time to Care*

They've tied the knot, but will their love last the distance?

*A Time to Abide*

When grief hovers like a cloud, will the sun ever shine again for Wendy?

*A Time to Rejoice*

He's never forgiven himself for the accident that killed his mother. Can he find forgiveness and true love?

### Transformed by Love Christian Romance Series

*Because We Loved*

*Because We Forgave*

*Because We Dreamed*

*Because We Believed*

*Because We Cared*

## Billionaires with Heart Series

*Her Kind-Hearted Billionaire*

A reluctant billionaire, a grieving young woman, and the trip *that changes their lives forever...*

*Her Generous Billionaire*

A grieving billionaire, a devoted solo mother, and a woman determined to sabotage their relationship...

*Her Disgraced Billionaire*

A billionaire in jail, a nurse who cares, and the challenge that changes their lives forever...

*Her Compassionate Billionaire*

A widowed billionaire with three young children. A replacement nanny who helps change his life...

## The Potter's House Books...

**Stories of hope, redemption, and second chances.**

*The Homecoming*

Can she surrender a life of fame and fortune to find true love?

*Unchained*

Imprisoned by greed — redeemed by love.

*Blessings of Love*

She's going on mission to help others. He's going to win her heart.

*The Hope We Share*

Can the Master Potter work in Rachel and Andrew's hearts and give them a second chance at love?

*The Love Abounds*

Can the Master Potter work in Megan's heart and save her marriage?

*Love's Healing Touch*

A doctor in need of healing. A nurse in need of love.

*Melody of Love*

She's fleeing an abusive relationship, he's grieving his wife's death…

*Whispers of Hope*

He's struggling to accept his new normal. She's losing her patience…

*Promise of Peace*

She's disillusioned and troubled. He has a secret…

**Heroes Of Eastbrooke Christian Suspense Series**

*Safe in His Arms*

SOME SAY HE'S HIDING. HE SAYS HE'S SURVIVING

*Under His Watch*

HE'LL STOP AT NOTHING TO PROTECT THOSE HE LOVES.
NOTHING.

*Within His Sight*

SHE'LL STOP AT NOTHING TO GET A STORY. HE'LL SCALE
THE HIGHEST MOUNTAIN TO RESCUE HER.

*Freed by His Love*

HE'S DRIVEN AND DETERMINED. SHE'S BROKEN AND
SCARED.

**Stand Alone Christian Romantic Suspense**

***Leave Before He Kills You***

When his face grew angry, I knew he could murder…

## The Madeleine Richards Series

Although the 3 book series is intended mainly for pre-teen/Middle Grade girls, it's been read and enjoyed by people of all ages. Here's what one reader had to say about it: *"Juliette has a fabulous way of bringing her characters to life. Maddy is at typical teenager with authentic views and actions that truly make it feel like you are feeling her pain and angst."* Reader

**Connect with Juliette:**

Email: author@julietteduncan.com

Website: www.julietteduncan.com

Facebook: www.facebook.com/JulietteDuncanAuthor

Twitter: https://twitter.com/Juliette_Duncan